Why had she nam[ed] him? *Unless...*

Dare couldn't breathe. His entire body shook with the force of the one question that immediately torpedoed through his brain.

He met her gaze and saw the look of guilt in her eyes and knew. Yet he had to have it confirmed. On unsteady legs, he crossed the room to stand in front of Shelly. He deftly grasped her elbow and brought her closer to him. So close he could see the dark irises of her eyes.

"You were two months pregnant when we broke up?" he asked in a pained whisper.

"Yes," she answered, snatching her arm from his hold.

"I have a son?"

Dare's face etched into tight lines as he stared at her. "How dare you! Who gave you the right, Shelly?"

"My love for you gave me the right, Dare," she said.

BRENDA JACKSON

is a die "heart" romantic who married her child-hood sweetheart and still proudly wears the "going steady" ring he gave her when she was fifteen. Because she's always believed in the power of love, Brenda's stories always have happy endings. In her real-life love story, Brenda and her husband of thirty-three years live in Jacksonville, Florida, and have two sons.

A *USA TODAY* bestselling author of over thirty romance titles, Brenda divides her time between family, writing and working in management at a major insurance company. You may write Brenda at P.O. Box 28267, Jacksonville, Florida 32226, her e-mail address at WriterBJackson@aol.com, or visit her Web site at www.brendajackson.net.

BRENDA JACKSON

A LITTLE DARE

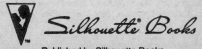

Published by Silhouette Books

America's Publisher of Contemporary Romance

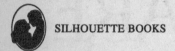

SILHOUETTE BOOKS

ISBN 0-373-81107-1

A LITTLE DARE

Copyright © 2003 by Brenda Streater Jackson

Visit Silhouette Books at www.eHarlequin.com

Printed in U.S.A.

To Pauline Hall, thanks for your feedback on the book in progress and for falling in love with Dare.

And most importantly, thanks to my Heavenly Father who gave me the gift to write.

Prologue

The son Dare Westmoreland didn't know he had, needed him.

Shelly Brockman knew that admission was long overdue as she stood in the living room of the house that had been her childhood home. The last box had been carried in and now the task of unpacking awaited her. Even with everything she faced, she felt good about being back in a place that filled her with many fond memories. Her thoughts were cut short with the slamming of the front door. She turned and met her son's angry expression.

"I'm going to hate it here!" He all but screamed at the top of his lungs. "I want to go back to Los Angeles! No matter what you say, this will never be my home!"

Shelly winced at his words and watched as he threw down the last bag filled with his belongings before racing up the stairs. Instead of calling after him, she closed her eyes, remembering why she had made the move from Cal-

ifornia to Georgia, and knew that no matter how AJ felt,
the move was the best thing for him. For the past year he
had been failing in school and hanging out with the wrong
crowd. Because of his height, he looked older than a ten-
year-old and had begun associating with an older group of
boys at school, those known to be troublemakers.

Her parents, who had retired and moved to Florida years
ago, had offered her the use of her childhood home rent-
free. As a result, she had made three of the hardest decisions of her life. First, deciding to move back to College
Park, Georgia, second switching from being a nurse who
worked inside the hospital to a home healthcare nurse, and
finally letting Dare Westmoreland know he had a son.

More than anything she hoped Dare would understand
that she had loved him too much to stand between him and
his dream of becoming an FBI agent all those years ago. Her
decision, unselfish as it had been, had cost AJ the chance to
know his father and Dare the chance to know his son.

Crossing the room she picked up AJ's bag. He was upset
about leaving his friends and moving to a place he considered Hicksville, USA. However, his attitude was the least
of her worries.

She sighed deeply and rubbed her forehead, knowing
she couldn't put off telling Dare much longer since chances
were he would hear she'd return to town. Besides, if he took
a good hard look at AJ, he would know the truth, and the
secret she had harbored for ten years would finally be out.

Deep within her heart she knew that it was time.

One

Sheriff Dare Westmoreland leaned forward in the chair behind his desk. From the defiant look on the face of the boy standing in front of him he could tell it would be one of those days. "Look, kid, I'm only going to ask you one more time. What is your name?"

The boy crossed his arms over his chest and had the nerve to glare at him and say, "And I've told you that I don't like cops and have no intention of giving you my name or anything else. And if you don't like it, arrest me."

Dare stood to his full height of six-feet-four, feeling every bit of his thirty-six years as he came from behind his desk to stare at the boy. He estimated the kid, who he'd caught throwing rocks at passing cars on the highway, to be around twelve or thirteen. It had been a long time since any kid living in his jurisdiction had outright sassed him. None of them would have dared, so it stood to reason that the kid was probably new in town.

"You will get your wish. Since you won't cooperate and tell me who you are, I'm officially holding you in police custody until someone comes to claim you. And while you're waiting you may as well make yourself useful. You'll start by mopping out the bathroom on the first floor, so follow me."

Dare shook his head, thinking he didn't envy this kid's parents one bit.

Shelly had barely brought her car to a complete stop in front of the sheriff's office before she was out of it. It had taken her a good two hours in Atlanta's heavy traffic to make it home after receiving word that AJ had not shown up at school, only to discover he wasn't at home. When it had started getting late she had gotten worried and called the police. After giving the dispatcher a description of AJ, the woman assured her that he was safe in their custody and that the reason she had not been contacted was because AJ had refused to give anyone his name. Without asking for any further details Shelly had jumped into her car and headed for the police station.

She let out a deep sigh. If AJ hadn't given anyone his name that meant the sheriff was not aware she was AJ's mother and for the moment that was a comforting thought. As she pushed open the door, she knew all her excuses for not yet meeting with Dare and telling him the truth had run out, and fate had decided to force her hand.

She was about to come face to face with Sheriff Dare Westmoreland.

"Sheriff, the parent of John Doe has arrived."

Dare looked up from the papers he was reading and

met his secretary's gaze. "Only one parent showed up, Holly?"

"Yes, just the mother. She's not wearing a wedding ring so I can only assume there isn't a father. At least not one that's around."

Dare nodded. "What's the kid doing now?" he asked, pushing the papers he'd been reading aside.

"He's out back watching Deputy McKade clean up his police motorcycle"

Dare nodded. "Send the woman in, Holly. I need to have a long talk with her. Her son needs a lot more discipline than he's evidently getting at home."

Dare moved away from his desk to stand at the window where he could observe the boy as he watched McKade polish his motorcycle. He inhaled deeply. There was something about the boy that he found oddly familiar. Maybe he reminded him of himself and his four brothers when they'd been younger. Although they had been quite a handful for their parents, headstrong and in some ways stubborn, they had known just how far to take it and just how much they could get away with. And they'd been smart enough to know when to keep their mouths closed. This kid had a lot to learn.

"Sheriff Westmoreland, this is Ms. Rochelle Brockman."

Dare swung his head around and his gaze collided with the woman he'd once loved to distraction. Suddenly his breath caught, his mouth went dry and every muscle in his body froze as memories rushed through his spiraling mind.

He could vividly recall the first time they'd met, their first kiss and the first time they had made love. The last time stood out in his mind now. He dragged his gaze from her face to do a total sweep of her body before returning to her face again. A shiver of desire tore through him, and he was glad that his position, standing behind his desk, blocked a view of his body from the waist down. Otherwise both women would have seen the arousal pressing against the zipper of his pants.

His gaze moved to her dark-brown hair, and he noted that it was shorter and cut in one of those trendy styles that accented the creamy chocolate coloring of her face as well as the warm brandy shade of her eyes.

The casual outfit she wore, a printed skirt and a matching blouse, made her look stylish, comfortable and ultra-feminine. Then there were the legs he still considered the most gorgeous pair he'd ever seen. Legs he knew could wrap around his waist while their bodies meshed in pleasure.

A deep sigh escaped his closed lips as he concluded that at thirty-three she was even more beautiful than he remembered and still epitomized everything feminine. They'd first met when she was sixteen and a sophomore in high school. He'd been nineteen, a few weeks shy of twenty and a sophomore in college, and had come home for a visit to find her working on a school project with his brother Stone. He had walked into the house at the exact moment she'd been leaning over Stone, explaining some scientific formula and wearing the sexiest pair of shorts he had ever seen on a female. He had thought she had a pair of legs that were simply a complete turn-on. When she had glanced up, noticed him staring and smiled, he'd been a goner. Never before had he been so aware of a woman. An immediate attraction had flared between them, holding him hostage to desires he'd never felt before.

After making sure Stone didn't have designs on her himself, he had made his move. And it was a move he'd never regretted making. They began seriously dating a few months later and had continued to do so for six long years, until he had made the mistake of ending things between them. Now it seemed the day of reckoning had arrived.

"Shelly."

"Dare."

It was as if the years had not passed between them, Dare suddenly thought. That same electrical charge the two of them always generated ignited full force, sending a high voltage searing through the room.

He cleared his throat. "Holly, you can leave me and Ms. Brockman alone now, " he thought it best to say.

His secretary looked at Shelly then back at him. "Sure, Sheriff," she murmured, and walked out of the office, pulling the door shut behind her.

Once the door closed, Dare turned his full attention back to Shelly. His gaze went immediately to her lips; lips he used to enjoy tasting time and time again; lips that were hot, sweet and ultra-responsive. One night he had thrust her into an orgasm just from gnawing on her lips and caressing them with the tip of his tongue.

He swallowed to get his bearings when he felt his body began responding to just being in the same room with her. He then admitted what he'd known for years. Shelly Brockman would always be the beginning and the end of his most blatant desires and a part of him could not believe she was back in College Park after being gone for so long.

Shelly felt the intensity of Dare's gaze and struggled to keep her emotions in check, but he was so disturbingly gorgeous that she found it hard to do so. Wearing his blue uniform, he still had that look that left a woman's mind whirling and her body overheated.

He had changed a lot from the young man she had fallen in love with years ago. He was taller, bigger and more muscular. The few lines he had developed in the corners of his eyes, and the firmness of his jaw made his face more angular, his coffee-colored features stark and disturbingly handsome and still a pleasure to look at.

She noted there were certain things about him that had remained the same. The shape of his mouth was still a total turn-on, and he still had those sexy dimples he used to flash at her so often. Then there were those dark eyes—deep, penetrating—that at one time had had the ability to read her mind by just looking at her. How else had he known when she'd wanted him to make love to her without her having to utter a single word?

Suddenly Shelly felt nervous, panicky when she remembered the reason she had moved back to town. But there was no way she could tell Dare that he was AJ's father—at least not today. She needed time to pull herself together. Seeing him again had derailed her senses, making it impossible for her to think straight. The only thing she wanted was to get AJ and leave.

"I came for my son, Dare," she finally found her voice to say, and even to her own ears it sounded wispy.

Dare let out a deep breath. It seemed she wanted to get right down to business and not dwell on the past. He had no intention of letting her do that, mainly because of what they had once meant to each other. "It's been a long time, Shelly. How have you been?" he asked raspily, failing to keep his own voice casual. He found the scent of her perfume just as sexy and enticing as the rest of her.

"I've been fine, Dare. How about you?"

"Same here."

She nodded. "Now may I see my son?"

Her insistence on keeping things non-personal was beginning to annoy the hell out of him. His eyes narrowed and his gaze zeroed in on her mouth; bad timing on his part. She nervously swiped her bottom lip with her tongue, causing his body to react immediately. He remembered that tongue and some of the things he had taught her to do with it. He dragged air into his lungs when he felt his muscles tense. "Aren't you going to ask why he's here?" he asked, his voice sounding tight, just as tight as his entire body felt.

She shrugged. "I assumed that since the school called and said he didn't show up today, one of your officers had picked him up for playing hooky."

"No, that's not it," he said, thinking that was a reasonable assumption to make. "I'm the one who picked him up, but he was doing something a bit more serious than playing hooky."

Shelly's eyes widened in alarm. "What?"

"I caught him throwing rocks at passing motorists on Old National Highway. Do you know what could have happened had a driver swerved to avoid getting hit?"

Shelly swallowed as she nodded. "Yes." The first thought that came to her mind was that AJ was in need of serious punishment, but she'd tried punishing him in the past and it hadn't seemed to work.

"I'm sorry about this, Dare," she apologized, not knowing what else to say. "We moved to town a few weeks ago and it hasn't been easy for him. He needs time to adjust."

Dare snorted. "From the way he acted in my office earlier today, I think what he needs is an attitude adjustment as well as a lesson in respect and manners. Whose kid is he anyway?"

Shelly straightened her spine. The mother in her took offense at his words. She admitted she had spoiled AJ somewhat, but still, considering the fact that she was a single parent doing the best she could, she didn't need Dare of all people being so critical. "He's my child."

Dare stared at her wondering if she really expected him to believe that. There was no way the kid could be hers, since in his estimation of the kid's age, she was a student in college and his steady girl about the same time the boy was born. "I mean who does he really belong to since I know you didn't have a baby twelve or thirteen years ago, Shelly."

Her gaze turned glacial. "He *is* mine, Dare. I gave birth to him *ten* years ago. He just looks older than he really is because of his height." Shelly watched Dare's gaze sharpen and darken, then his brows pulled together in a deep, furious frown.

"What the hell do you mean *you* gave birth to him?" he asked, a shocked look on his face and a tone of voice that bordered on anger and total disbelief.

She met his glare with one of her own. "I meant just what I said. Now may I see him?" She made a move to leave Dare's office but he caught her arm.

"Are you saying that he was born after you left here?"

"Yes."

Dare released her. His features had suddenly turned to stone, and the gaze that focused on hers was filled with hurt and pain. "It didn't take you long to find someone in California to take my place after we broke up, did it?"

His words were like a sharp, painful slap to Shelly's face. He thought that she had given birth to someone else's child! How could he think that when she had loved him so much? She was suddenly filled with extreme anger. "Why does it matter to you what I did after I left here, Dare, when you decided after six long years that you wanted a career with the FBI more than you wanted me?"

Dare closed his eyes, remembering that night and what he had said to her, words he had later come to regret. He slowly reopened his eyes and looked at her. She appeared just as stricken now as she had then. He doubted he would ever forget the deep look of hurt on her face that night he had told her that he wanted to break up with her to pursue a career with the FBI.

"Shelly, I..."

"No, Dare. I think we've said enough, too much in fact. Just let me get my son and go home."

Dare inhaled deeply. It was too late for whatever he wanted to say to her. Whatever had once been between them was over and done with. Turning, he slowly walked back over to his desk. "There's some paperwork that needs to be completed before you can take him with you. Since he refused to provide us with any information, we couldn't do it earlier."

He read the question that suddenly flashed in her gaze and said. "And no, this will not be a part of any permanent record, although I think it won't be such a bad idea for him to come back every day this week after school for an hour to do additional chores, especially since he mentioned he's not into any after-school activity. The light tasks I'll be assigning to him will work off some of that rebellious energy he has."

He met her gaze. "However, if this happens again, Shelly, he'll be faced with having to perform hours of community service as well as getting slapped with a juvenile delinquent record. Is that understood?"

She nodded, feeling much appreciative. Had he wanted to, Dare could have handled things a lot more severely. What AJ had done was a serious offense. "Yes, I understand, and I want to thank you."

She sighed deeply. It seemed fate would not be forcing her hand today after all. She had a little more time before having to tell Dare the truth.

Dare sat down at his desk with a form in front of him and a pen in his hand. "Now then, what's his name?"

Shelly swallowed deeply. "AJ Brockman."

"I need his real name."

She couldn't open her mouth to get the words out. It seemed fate wouldn't be as gracious as she'd thought after all.

Dare was looking down at the papers in front of him, however, the pause went on so long he glanced up and looked at her. He had known Shelly long enough to know when she was nervous about something. His eyes narrowed as he wondered what her problem was.

"What's his real name, Shelly?" he repeated.

He watched as she looked away briefly. Returning her gaze she stared straight into his eyes and without blinking said. "Alisdare Julian Brockman."

Two

Air suddenly washed from Dare's lung as if someone had cut off the oxygen supply in the room and he couldn't breathe. Everything started spinning around him and he held on to his desk with a tight grip. However, that didn't work since his hands were shaking worse than a volcano about to explode. In fact his entire body shook with the force of the one question that immediately torpedoed through his brain. Why would she name her son after him? Unless . .

He met her gaze and saw the look of guilt in her eyes and knew. Yet he had to have it confirmed. He stood on non-steady legs and crossed the room to stand in front of Shelly. He grasped her elbow and brought her closer to him, so close he could see the dark irises of her eyes.

"When is his birth date?" he growled, quickly finding his equilibrium.

Shelly swallowed so deeply she knew for certain Dare

could see her throat tighten, but she refused to let his re-action unsettle her any more than it had. She lifted her chin. "November twenty-fifth."

He flinched, startled. "Two months?" he asked in a pained whisper yet with intense force. "You were two months pregnant when we broke up?"

She snatched her arm from his hold. "Yes."

Anger darkened the depths of his eyes then flared through his entire body at the thought of what she had kept from him. "I have a son?"

Though clearly upset, he had asked the question so quietly that Shelly could only look at him. For a long moment she didn't answer, but then she knew that in spite of everything between them, there was never a time she had not been proud that AJ was Dare's son. That was the reason she had returned to College Park, because she felt it was time he was included in AJ's life. "Yes, you have a son."

"But—but I didn't know about him!"

His words were filled with trembling fury and she knew she had to make him understand. "I found out I was pregnant the day before my graduation party and had planned to tell you that night. But before I got the chance you told me about the phone call you'd received that day, offering you a job with the Bureau and how much you wanted to take it. I loved you too much to stand in your way, Dare. I knew that telling you I was pregnant would have changed everything, and I couldn't do that to you."

Dare's face etched into tight lines as he stared at her. "And you made that decision on your own?"

She nodded. "Yes."

"How dare you! Who in the hell gave you the right to do that, Shelly?"

She felt her own anger rise. "It's not who but what. My love for you gave me the right, Dare," she said and without giving him a chance to say another word, she angrily walked out of his office.

Fury consumed Dare at a degree he had never known before and all he could do was stand there, rooted in place, hell-shocked at what he had just discovered.

He had a son.

He crossed the room and slammed his fist hard on the desk. Ten years! For ten years she had kept it from him. Ten solid years.

Ignoring the pain he felt in his hand, he breathed in deeply when it hit him that he was the father of John Doe. No, she'd called him AJ but she had named him Alisdare Julian. He took a deep, calming breath. For some reason she had at least done that. His son did have his name—at least part of it anyway. Had he known, his son would also be wearing the name Westmoreland, which was rightfully his.

Dare slowly walked over to the window and looked out, suddenly seeing the kid through different eyes—a father's eyes, and his heart and soul yearned for a place in his son's life; a place he rightly deserved. And from the way the kid had behaved earlier it was a place Dare felt he needed to be. It seemed that Alisdare Julian Brockman was a typical Westmoreland male—headstrong and stubborn as hell. As Dare studied him through the windowpane, he could see Westmoreland written all over him and was surprised he hadn't seen it earlier.

He turned when the buzzer sounded on his desk. He took the few steps to answer it. "Yes, Holly?"

"Ms. Brockman is ready to leave, sir. Have you completed the paperwork?"

Dare frowned as he glanced down at the half-completed form on his desk. "No, I haven't."

"What do you want me to tell her, Sheriff?"

Dare sighed. If Shelly for one minute thought she could just walk out of here and take their son, she had another thought coming. There was definitely unfinished business between them. "Tell Ms. Brockman there're a few things I need to take care of. After which, I'll speak with her again in my office. In the meantime, she's not to see her son."

There was a slight pause before Holly replied. "Yes, sir."

After hanging up the phone Dare picked up the form that contained all the standard questions, however, he didn't know any answers about his son. He wondered if he could ever forgive Shelly for doing that to him. No matter what she said, she had no right to have kept him in the dark about his son for ten years.

After the elder Brockmans had retired and moved away, there had been no way to stay in touch except for Ms. Kate, the owner of Kate's Diner who'd been close friends with Shelly's mother. But no matter how many times he had asked Kate about the Brockmans, specifically Shelly, she had kept a stiff lip and a closed mouth.

A number of the older residents in town who had kept an eye on his and Shelly's budding romance during those six years had been pretty damn disappointed with the way he had ended things between them. Even his family, who'd thought the world of Shelly, had decided he'd had a few screws loose for breaking up with her.

He sighed deeply. As sheriff, he of all people should have known she had returned to College Park; he made it his business to keep up with all the happenings around town. She must have come back during the time he had been busy apprehending those two fugitives who'd been hiding out in the area.

With the form in one hand he picked up the phone with the other. His cousin, Jared Westmoreland, was the attorney in the family and Dare felt the need for legal advice.

"The sheriff needs to take care of few things and would like to see you again in his office when he's finished."

Shelly nodded but none to happily. "Is there anyway I can see my son?"

The older woman shook her head. "I'm sorry but you can't see or talk to him until the sheriff completes the paperwork."

When the woman walked off Shelly shook her head. What had taken place in Dare's office had certainly not been the way she'd envisioned telling him about AJ. She walked over to a chair and sat down, wondering how long would it be before she could get AJ and leave. Dare was calling the shots and there wasn't anything she could do about it but wait. She knew him well enough to know that anger was driving him to strike back at her for what she'd done, what she'd kept from him. A part of her wondered if he would ever forgive her for doing what she'd done, although at the time she'd thought it was for the best.

"Ms. Brockman?"

Shelly shifted her gaze to look into the face of a uniformed man who appeared to be in his late twenties. "Yes?"

"I'm Deputy Rick McKade, and the sheriff wants to see you now."

Shelly stood. She wasn't ready for another encounter with Dare, but evidently he was ready for another one with her.

"All right."

This time when she entered Dare's office he was sitting behind his desk with his head lowered while writing something. She hoped it was the paperwork she needed to get AJ and go home, but a part of her knew the moment Dare lifted his head and looked up at her, that he would not make things easy on her. He was still angry and very much upset.

"Shelly?"

She blinked when she realized Dare had been talking. She also realized Deputy McKade had left and closed the door behind him. "I'm sorry, what did you say?"

He gazed at her for a long moment. "I said you could have a seat."

She shook her head. "I don't want to sit down, Dare. All I want is to get AJ and take him home."

"Not until we talk."

She took a deep breath and felt a tightness in her throat. She also felt tired and emotionally drained. "Can we make arrangements to talk some other time, Dare?"

Shelly regretted making the request as soon as the words had left her mouth. They had pushed him, not over the edge but just about. He stood and covered the distance separating them. The degree of anger on his face actually had her taking a step back. She didn't ever recall seeing him so furious.

"Talk some other time? You have some nerve even to suggest something like that. I just found out that I have a son, a ten-year-old son, and you think you can just waltz back into town with my child and expect me to turn my head and look away and not claim what's mine?"

Shelly released the breath she'd been holding, hearing the sound of hurt and pain in Dare's voice. "No, I never thought any of those things, Dare," she said softly. "In fact, I thought just the opposite, which is why I moved back. I knew once I told you about AJ that you would claim him as yours. And I also knew you would help me save him."

Eyes narrowed and jaw tight, Dare stared at her. She watched as immediate concern—a father's concern—appear in his gaze. "Save him from what?"

"Himself."

She paused, then answered the question she saw flaring

in his eyes. "You've met him, and I'm sure you saw how angry he is. I can only imagine what sort of an impression he made on you today, but deep down he's really a good kid, Dare. I began putting in extra hours at the hospital, which resulted in him spending more time with sitters and finding ways to get into trouble, especially at school when he got mixed up with the wrong crowd. That's the reason I moved back here, to give him a fresh start—with your help."

Anger, blatant and intense, flashed in Dare's eyes. "Are you saying that the only reason you decided to tell me about him and seek my help was because he'd started giving you trouble? What about those years when he was a *good* kid? Did you not think I had a right to know about his existence then?"

Shelly held his gaze. "I thought I was doing the right thing by not telling you about him, Dare."

A muscle worked in his jaw. "Well, you were wrong. You didn't do the right thing. Nothing would have been more important to me than being a father to my son, Shelly."

A twinge of regret, a fleeting moment of sadness for the ten years of fatherhood she had taken away from him touched Shelly. She had to make him understand why she had made the decision she had that night. "That night you stood before me and said that becoming a FBI agent was all you had ever wanted, Dare, all you had ever dreamed about, and that the reason we couldn't be together any longer was because of the nature of the work. You felt it was best that as an agent, you shouldn't have a wife or family." She blinked back tears when she added. "You even said you were glad I hadn't gotten pregnant any of those times we had made love."

She wiped at her eyes. "How do you think I felt hearing you say that, two months pregnant and knowing that our baby and I stood in the way of you having what you desired most?"

When AJ's laughter floated in from the outside, Shelly slowly walked over to the window and looked into the yard below. The boy was watching a uniformed officer give a police dog a bath. This was the first time she had heard AJ laugh in months, and the sheer look of enjoyment on his face at that moment was priceless. She turned back around to face Dare, knowing she had to let him know how she felt.

"When I found out I was pregnant there was no question in my mind that I wouldn't tell you, Dare. In fact, I had been anxiously waiting all that night for the perfect time to do so. And then as soon as we were alone, you dropped the bomb on me."

She inhaled deeply before continuing. "For six long years I assumed that I had a definite place in your heart. I had actually thought that I was the most important thing to you, but in less than five minutes you proved I was wrong. Five minutes was all it took for you to wash six years down the drain when you told me you wanted your freedom."

She stared down at the hardwood floor for a moment before meeting his gaze again. "Although you didn't love me anymore, I still wanted our child. I knew that telling you about my pregnancy would cause you to forfeit your dream and do what you felt was the honorable thing—spend the rest of your life in a marriage you didn't want."

She quickly averted her face so he wouldn't see her tears. She didn't want him to know how much he had hurt her ten years ago. She didn't want him to see that the scars hadn't healed; she doubted they ever would.

"Shelly?"

The tone that called her name was soft, gentle and tender. So tender that she glanced up at him, finding it difficult to meet his dark, piercing gaze, though she met it anyway. She fought the tremble in her voice when she said, "What?"

"That night, I never said I didn't love you," he said, his voice low, a near-whisper. "How could you have possibly thought that?"

She shook her head sadly and turned more fully toward him, not believing he had asked the question. "How could I not think it, Dare?"

Her response made him raise a thick eyebrow. Yes, how could she not think it? He had broken off with her that night, never thinking she would assume that he had never loved her or that she hadn't meant everything to him. Now he could see how she could have felt that way.

He inhaled deeply and rubbed a hand over his face, wondering how he could explain things to her when he really didn't understand himself. He knew he had to try anyway. "It seems I handled things very poorly that night," he said.

Shelly chuckled softly and shrugged her shoulders. "It depends on what you mean by poorly. I think that you accomplished what you set out to do, Dare. You got rid of a girlfriend who stood between you and your career plans."

"That wasn't it, Shelly."

"Then tell me what was *it*," she said, trying to hold on to the anger she was beginning to feel all over again.

For a few moments he didn't say anything, then he spoke. "I loved you, Shelly, and the magnitude of what I felt for you began to frighten me because I knew what you and everyone else expected of me. But a part of me knew that although I loved you, I wasn't ready to take the big step and settle down with the responsibility of a wife. I also knew there was no way I could ask you to wait for me any longer. We had already dated six years and everyone—my family, your family and this whole damn town—expected us to get married. It was time. We had both finished college and I had served a sufficient amount of time in the marines, and you were about to embark on a career in nursing. There was no way I could ask you to wait around and twiddle your thumbs while I worked as an agent. It wouldn't have been fair. You deserved more. You deserved better. So I thought the best thing to do was to give you your freedom."

Shelly dipped her chin, no longer able to look into his eyes. Moments later she lifted her gaze to meet his. "So, I'm not the only one who made a decision about us that night."

Dare inhaled deeply, realizing she was right. Just as she'd done, he had made a decision about them. A few moments later he said. "I wish I had handled things differently, Shelly. Although I loved you, I wasn't ready to become the husband I knew you wanted."

"Yet you want me to believe you would have been ready to become a father?" she asked softly, trying to make him see reason. "All I knew after that night was that the man I loved no longer wanted me, and that his dream wasn't a future with me but one in law enforcement. And I loved him enough to step aside to let him fulfill that dream. That's the reason I left without telling you about the baby, Dare. That's the only reason."

He nodded. "Had I known you were pregnant, my dreams would not have mattered at that point."

"Yes, I knew that better than anyone."

Dare finally understood the point she'd been trying to make and sighed at how things had turned out for them. Ten years ago he'd thought that becoming a FBI agent was the ultimate. It had taken seven years of moving from place to place, getting burnt-out from undercover operations, waking each morning cloaked in danger and not knowing if his next assignment would be his last, to finally make him realize the career that had once been his dream had turned into a living nightmare. Resigning from the Bureau, he had returned home to open up a security firm about the same time Sheriff Dean Whitlow, who'd been in office since Dare was in his early teens, had decided to retire. It was Sheriff Whitlow who had talked him into running for the position he was about to vacate, saying that with Dare's experience, he was the best man for the job. Now, after three years at it, Dare had forged a special bond with the town he'd always loved and the people he'd known all of his life. And compared to what he had done as an FBI agent, being sheriff was a gravy train.

He glanced out of the window and didn't say anything for the longest time as he watched AJ. Then he spoke. "I take it that he doesn't know anything about me."

Shelly shook her head. "No. Years ago I told him that his father was a guy I had loved and thought I would marry, but that things didn't work out and we broke up. I told him I moved away before I had a chance to tell him I was pregnant."

Dare stared at her. "That's it?"

"Yes, that's it. He was fairly young at the time, but occasionally as he got older, he would ask if I knew how to reach you if I ever wanted to, and I told him yes and that if he ever wanted me to contact you I would. All he had to do was ask, but he never has."

Dare nodded. "I want him to know I'm his father, Shelly."

"I want him to know you're his father, too, Dare, but we need to approach this lightly with him," she whispered softly "He's going through enough changes right now, and I don't want to get him any more upset than he already is. I have an idea as to how and when we can tell him, and I hope after hearing me out that you'll agree."

Dare went back to his desk. "All right, so what do you suggest?"

Shelly nodded and took a seat across from his desk. She held her breath, suddenly feeling uncomfortable telling him what she thought was the best way to handle AJ. She knew her son's emotional state better than anyone. Right now he was mad at the world in general and her in particular, because she had taken him out of an environment he'd grown comfortable with, although that environment as far as she was concerned, had not been a healthy one for a ten-year-old. His failing grades and the trouble he'd gotten into had proven that.

"What do you suggest, Shelly?" Dare asked again, sitting down and breaking into her thoughts.

Shelly cleared her throat. "I know how anxious you are to have AJ meet you, but I think it would be best, considering everything, if he were to get to know you as a friend before knowing you as his father."

Dare frowned, not liking the way her suggestion sounded. "But I am his father, Shelly, not his friend."

"Yes, and that's the point. More than anything, AJ needs a friend right now, Dare, someone he can trust and connect with. He has a hard time making friends, which is why he began hanging out with the wrong type of kids at the school he attended in California. They readily accepted him for all the wrong reasons. I've talked to a few of his teachers since moving here and he's having the same problems. He's just not outgoing."

Dare nodded. Of the five Westmoreland brothers, he was the least outgoing, if you didn't count Thorn who was known to be a pain in the butt at times. Growing up, Dare had felt that his brothers were all the playmates he had needed, and because of that, he never worried about making friends or being accepted. His brothers were his friends—his best friends—and as far as he'd been concerned they were enough. It was only after he got older and his brothers began seeking other interests that he began getting out more, playing sports, meeting people and making new friends.

So if AJ wasn't as outgoing as most ten-year-old kids, he had definitely inherited that characteristic from him. "So how do you think I should handle it?"

"I suggest that we don't tell him the truth about you just yet, and that you take the initiative to form a bond with him, share his life and get to know him."

Dare raised a dark brow. "And just how am I supposed to do that? Our first meeting didn't exactly get off to a great start, Shelly. Technically, I arrested him, for heaven's sake. My own son! A kid who didn't bat an eye when he informed me he hated cops—which is what I definitely am. Then there's this little attitude problem of his that I feel needs adjusting. So come on, let's be real here. How am I supposed to develop a relationship with *my kid* when he dislikes everything I stand for?"

Shelly shook her head. "He doesn't really hate cops, Dare, he just thinks he does because of what happened as we were driving from California to here."

Dare lifted a brow. "What happened?"

"I got pulled over in some small Texas town and the officer was extremely rude. Needless to say he didn't make a good impression on AJ."

She sighed deeply. "But you can change that, Dare. That's why I think the two of you getting together and developing a relationship as friends first would be the ideal thing. Ms. Kate told me that you work with the youth in the community and about the Little League baseball team that you coach. I want to do whatever it takes to get AJ involved in something like that."

"And he can become involved as my son."

"I think we should go the friendship route first, Dare."

Dare shook his head. "Shelly, you haven't thought this through. I understand what you're saying because I know how it was for me as a kid growing up. At least I had my brothers who were my constant companions. But I think you've forgotten one very important thing here."

Shelly raised her brow. "What?"

"Most of the people in College Park know you, and most of them have long memories. Once they hear that you have a ten-year-old son, they'll start counting months, and once they see him they'll definitely know the truth. They will see just how much of a Westmoreland he is. He favors my brothers and me. The reason I didn't see it before was because I wasn't looking for it. But you better believe the good people of this town will be. Once you're seen with AJ they'll be looking for anything to link me to him, and it will be easy for them to put two and two together. And don't let them find out that he was named after me. That will be the icing on the cake."

Dare gave her time to think about what he'd said before continuing. "What's going to happen if AJ learns that I'm his father from someone other than us? He'll resent us for keeping the truth from him."

Shelly sighed deeply, knowing Dare was right. It would be hard to keep the truth hidden in a close-knit town like College Park.

"But there is another solution that will accomplish the same purpose, Shelly," he said softly.

She met his gaze. "What?"

Dare didn't say anything at first, then he said. "I'm asking that you hear me out before jumping to conclusions and totally dishing the idea."

She stared at him before nodding her head. "All right."

Dare continued. "You said you told AJ that you and his father had planned to marry but that we broke up and you moved away before telling him you were pregnant, right?"

Shelly nodded. "Yes."

"And he knows this is the town you grew up in, right?"

"Yes, although I doubt he's made the connection."

"What if you take him into your confidence and let him know that his father lives here in College Park, then go a step further and tell him who I am, but convince him that you haven't told me yet and get his opinion on what you should do?"

Since Dare and AJ had already butted heads, Shelly had a pretty good idea of what he would want her to do—keep the news about him from Dare. He would be dead set against developing any sort of personal relationship with Dare, and she told Dare so.

"Yes, but what if he's placed in a position where he has to accept me, or has to come in constant contact with me?" Dare asked.

"How?"

"If you and I were to rekindle our relationship, at least pretend to do so."

Shelly frowned, clearly not following Dare. "And just how will that help the situation? Word will still get out that you're his father."

"Yes, but he'll already know the truth and he'll think I'm the one in the dark. He'll either want me to find out the truth or he'll hope that I don't. In the meantime I'll do my damnedest to win him over."

"And what if you can't?"

"I will. AJ needs to feel that he belongs, Shelly, and he does belong. Not only does he belong to you and to me, but he also belongs to my brothers, my parents and the rest of the Westmorelands. Once we start seeing each other again, he'll be exposed to my family, and I believe when that happens and I start developing a bond with him, he'll eventually want to acknowledge me as his father."

Dare shifted in his chair. "Besides," he added smiling. "If he really doesn't want us to get together, he'll be so busy thinking of ways to keep us apart that he won't have time to get into trouble."

Shelly lifted a brow, knowing Dare did have a point. However, she wasn't crazy about his plan, especially not the part she would play. The last thing she needed was to pretend they were falling in love all over again. Already, being around him was beginning to feel too comfortably familiar.

She sighed deeply. In order for Dare's plan to work, they would have to start spending time together. She couldn't help wondering how her emotions would be able to handle that. And she didn't even want to consider what his nearness might do to her hormones, since it had been a long time since she had spent any time with a man. A very long time.

She cleared her throat when she noticed Dare watching her intently and wondered if he knew what his gaze was doing to her. Biting her lower lip and shifting in her seat, she asked. "How do you think he's going to feel when he finds out that we aren't really serious about each other, and it was just a game we played to bring him around?"

"I think he'll accept the fact that although we aren't married, we're friends who like and respect each other. Most boys from broken relationships I come in contact with have parents who dislike each other. I think it's important that a child sees that although they aren't married, his parents are still friends who make his wellbeing their top priority."

Shelly shook her head. "I don't know, Dare. A lot can go wrong with what you're proposing."

"True, but on the other hand, a lot can go right. This way we're letting AJ call the shots, or at least we're letting him think that he is. This will give him what he'll feel is a certain degree of leverage, power and control over the situation. From working closely with kids, I've discovered that if you try forcing them to do something they will rebel. But if you sit tight and be patient, they'll eventually come around on their own. That's what I'm hoping will happen in this case. Chances are he'll resent me at first, but that's the chance I have to take. Winning him over will be my mission, Shelly, one I plan to accomplish. And trust me, it will be the most important mission of my life."

He studied her features, and when she didn't say anything for the longest time he said. "I have a lot more to lose than you, but I'm willing to risk it. I don't want to spend too much longer with my son not knowing who I am. At least this way he'll know that I'm his father, and it will be up to me to do everything possible to make sure that he wants to accept me in his life."

He inhaled deeply. "So will you at least think about what I've proposed?"

Shelly met his gaze. "Yes, Dare, I'll need time," she said quietly.

"Overnight. That's all the time I can give you, Shelly."

"But, I need more time."

Dare stood. "I can't give you any more time than that. I've lost ten years already and can't afford to lose any more. And just so you'll know, I've made plans to meet with Jared for lunch tomorrow. I'll ask him to act as my attorney so that I'll know my rights as AJ's father."

Shelly shook her head sadly. "There's no need for you to do that, Dare. I don't intend to keep you and AJ apart. As I said, you're the reason I returned."

Dare nodded. "Will you meet me for breakfast at Kate's

Diner in the morning so we can decide what we're going to do?"

Shelly felt she needed more time but knew there was no way Dare would give it to her. "All right. I'll meet you in the morning."

Three

Dare reached across his desk and hit the buzzer.

"Yes, sheriff?"

"McKade, please bring in John Doe."

Shelly frowned when she glanced over at Dare. "John Doe?"

Dare shrugged. "That's the usual name for any unidentified person we get in here, and since he refused to give us his name, we had no choice."

She nodded. "Oh."

Before Dare could say anything else, McKade walked in with AJ. The boy frowned when he saw his mother. "I wondered if you were ever going to come, Mom."

Shelly smiled wryly. "Of course I was going to come. Had you given them your name they would have called me sooner. You have a lot of explaining to do as to why you weren't in school today. It's a good thing Sheriff Westmoreland stopped you before you could cause harm to anyone."

AJ turned and glared at Dare. "Yeah, but I still don't like cops."

Dare crossed his arms on his chest. "And I don't like boys with bad attitudes. To be frank, it doesn't matter whether or not you like cops, but you'd sure better learn to respect them and what they stand for." This might be his son, Dare thought, but he intended to teach him a lesson in respect, starting now.

AJ turned to his mother. "I'm ready to go."

Shelly nodded. "All right."

"Not yet," Dare said, not liking the tone AJ had used with Shelly, or how easily she had given in to him. "What you did today was a serious matter, and as part of your punishment, I expect you to come back every day this week after school to do certain chores I'll have lined up for you."

"And if I don't show up?"

"AJ!"

Dare held up his hand, cutting off anything Shelly was about to say. This was between him and his son. "And if you don't show up, I'll know where to find you and when I do it will only make things a lot worse for you. Trust me."

Dare's gaze shifted to Shelly. This was not the way he wanted to start things off with his son, but he'd been left with little choice. AJ had to respect him as the sheriff as well as accept him as his father. From the look on Shelly's face he knew she understood that as well.

"Sheriff Westmoreland is right," she said firmly, giving Dare her support. "And you *will* show up after school to do whatever he has for you to do. Is that understood?"

"Yeah, yeah, I understand," the boy all but snapped. "Can we go now?"

Dare nodded and handed her the completed form. "I'll walk the two of you out to the car since I was about to leave anyway."

Once Shelly and AJ were in the car and had buckled up their seat belts, Dare glanced into the car and said to the boy, "I'll see you tomorrow when you get out of school."

Ignoring AJ's glare, he then turned and the look he gave Shelly said that he expected to see her tomorrow as well, at Kate's Diner in the morning. "Good night and drive safely."

He then walked away.

An hour later, Dare walked into a room where four men sat at a table engaged in a card game. The four looked up and his brother Stone spoke. "You're late."

"I had important business to take care of," Dare said grabbing a bottle of beer and leaning against the refrigerator in Stone's kitchen. "I'll wait this round out and just watch."

His brothers nodded as they continued with the game. Moments later, Chase Westmoreland let out a curse. Evidently he was losing as usual, Dare thought smiling. He then thought about how the four men at the table were more than just brothers to him; they were also his very best friends, although Thorn, the one known for his moodiness, could test that friendship and brotherly love to the limit at times. At thirty-five, Thorn was only eleven months younger than him, and built and raced motorcycles for a living. Last year he'd been the only African-American on the circuit.

His brother Stone, known for his wild imagination, had recently celebrated his thirty-third birthday and wrote action-thriller novels under the pen name, Rock Mason. Then there were the fraternal thirty-two-year-old twins, Chase and Storm. Chase was the oldest by seven minutes and owned a soul-food restaurant in downtown Atlanta, and Storm was the fireman in the family. According to their mother, she had gone into delivery unexpectedly while riding in the car with their Dad. When a bad storm had come up, he chased time and outran the storm to get her to the hospital. Thus she had named her last two sons Chase and Storm.

"You're quiet, Dare."

Dare looked up from studying his beer bottle and brought his thoughts back to the present. He met Stone's curious stare. "Is that a crime?"

Stone grinned. "No, but if it was a crime I'm sure you'd arrest yourself since you're such a dedicated lawman."

Chase chuckled. "Leave Dare alone. Nothing's wrong with him other than he's keeping Thorn company with this celibacy thing," he said jokingly.

"Shut up, Storm, before I hurt you," Thorn Westmoreland said, without cracking a smile.

Everyone knew Thorn refrained from having sex while preparing for a race, which accounted for his prickly mood most of the time. But since Thorn had been in the same mood for over ten months now they couldn't help but wonder what his problem was. Dare had a clue but decided not to say. He sighed and crossed the room and sat down at the table. "Guess who's back in town."

Storm looked up from studying his hand and grinned. "Okay, I'll play your silly guessing game. Who's back in town, Dare?"

"Shelly."

Everyone at the table got quiet as they looked up at him. Then Stone spoke. "*Our* Shelly?"

Dare looked at his brother and frowned. "No, not *our* Shelly, *my* Shelly."

Stone glared at him. "*Your* Shelly? You could have fooled us, the way you dumped her."

Dare leaned back in his chair. He'd known it was coming. His brothers had actually stopped speaking to him for weeks after he'd broken off with Shelly. "I did not dump her. I merely made the decision that I wasn't ready for marriage and wanted a career with the Bureau instead.

"That sounds pretty much like you dumped her to me," Stone said angrily. "You knew she was the marrying kind. And you led her to believe, like you did the rest of us, that the two of you would eventually marry when she finished college. In my book you played her for a fool, and I've always felt bad about it because I'm the one who introduced the two of you," he added, glaring at his brother.

Dare stood. "I did not play her for a fool. Why is it so hard to believe that I really loved her all those years?" he asked, clearly frustrated. He'd had this same conversation with Shelly earlier.

"Because," Thorn said slowly and in a menacing tone as he threw out a card, "I would think most men don't walk away from the woman they claim to love for no damn reason, especially not some lame excuse about not being ready to settle down. The way I see it, Dare, you wanted to have your cake and eat it too." He took a swig of his beer. "Let's change the subject before I get mad all over again and knock the hell out of you for hurting her the way you did."

Chase narrowed his eyes at Dare. "Yeah, and I hope she's happily married with a bunch of kids. It would serve you right for letting the best thing that ever happen to you get away."

Dare raised his eyes to the ceiling, wondering if there was such a thing as family loyalty when it came to Shelly Brockman. He decided to sit back down when a new card game began. "She isn't happily married with a bunch of kids, Chase, but she does have a son. He's ten."

Stone smiled happily. "Good for her. I bet it ate up your guts to know she got involved with someone else and had his baby after she left here."

Dare leaned back in his chair. "Yeah, I went through some pretty hard stomach pains until I found out the truth."

Storm raised a brow. "The truth about what?"

Dare smirked at each one of his brothers before answering. "Shelly's son is mine."

Early the next morning Dare walked into Kate's Diner.

"Good morning, Sheriff."

"Good morning, Boris. How's that sore arm doing?"

"Fine. I'll be ready to play you in another game of basketball real soon."

"I'm counting on it."

"Good morning, Sheriff."

"Good morning, Ms. Mamie. How's your arthritis?"

"A pain as usual," was the old woman's reply.

"Good morning, Sheriff Westmoreland."

"Good morning, Lizzie," Dare greeted the young waitress as he slid into the stool at the counter. She was old man Barton's granddaughter and was working at the diner part-time while taking classes at the college in town.

He smiled when Lizzie automatically poured his coffee. She knew just how he liked it. Black. "Where's Ms. Kate this morning?" he asked after taking a sip.

"She hasn't come in yet."

He raised a dark brow. For as long as he'd known Ms. Kate—and that had been all of his thirty-six years—he'd never known her to be late to work at the diner. "Is everything all right?"

"Yes, I guess so," Lizzie said, not looking the least bit worried. "She called and said Mr. Granger was stopping by her house this morning to take a look her hot-water heater. She thinks it's broken and wanted to be there when he arrived."

Dare nodded. It had been rumored around town for

years that old man Granger and Ms. Kate were sweet on each other.

"Would you like for me to go ahead and order your usual, Sheriff?"

He rolled his shoulders as if to ease sore muscles as he smiled up at her and said. "No, not yet. I'm waiting on someone." He glanced at his watch. "She should be here any minute."

Lizzie nodded. "All right then. I'll be back when your guest arrives."

Dare was just about to check his watch again when he heard the diner's door open behind him, followed by Boris's loud exclamation. "Well, my word, if it isn't Shelly Brockman! What on earth are you doing back here in College Park?"

Dare turned around on his stool as other patrons who'd known Shelly when she lived in town hollered out similar greetings. He had forgotten just how popular she'd been with everyone, both young and old. That was one of the reasons the entire town had all but skinned him alive when he'd broken off with her.

A muscle in his jaw twitched when he noticed that a few of the guys she'd gone to school with—Boris Jones, David Wright and Wayland Miller—who'd known years ago that she was off limits because of him, were checking her out now. And he could understand why. She looked pretty damn good, and she still had that natural ability to turn men on without even trying. Blue was a color she wore well and nothing about that had changed, he thought, as his gaze roamed over the blue sundress she was wearing. With thin straps tied at the shoulders, it was a decent length that stopped right above her knees and showed off long beautiful bare legs and feet encased in a pair of black sandals. When he felt his erection straining against the crotch of his pants, he knew he was in big trouble. He was beginning to feel a powerful and compelling need that he hadn't felt in a long time; at least ten years.

"Is that her, Sheriff? The woman you've been waiting on?"

Lizzie's question interrupted Dare's musings. "Yes, that's her."

"Will the two of you be sitting at the counter or will you be using a table or a booth?"

Now that's a loaded question, Dare thought. He wished—doubly so—that he could take Shelly and use a table or a booth. He could just imagine her spread out on either. He shook his head. Although he'd always been sexually attracted to Shelly, he'd never thought of her with so much lust before, and he couldn't help wondering why. Maybe it was because in the past she'd always been his. Now things were different, she was no longer his and he was lusting hard—and he meant hard!—for something he had lost.

"Sheriff?"

Knowing Lizzie was waiting for his decision, he glanced toward the back of the diner and made a quick decision. "We'll be sitting at a booth in the back." Once he was confident he had his body back under control, he stood and walked over to where Shelly was surrounded by a number of people, mostly men.

Breaking into their conversations he said. "Good morning, Shelly. Are you ready for breakfast?"

It seemed the entire diner got quiet and all eyes turned to him. The majority of those present remembered that he had been the one to break Shelly's heart, which ultimately had resulted in her leaving town, and from the way everyone was looking at him, the last thing they wanted was for her to become involved with him again.

In fact, old Mr. Sylvester turned to him and said. "I'm surprised Shelly is willing to give you the time of day, Sheriff, after what you did to her ten years ago."

"You got that right," eighty-year-old Mamie Potter agreed.

Dare rolled his eyes. That was all he needed, the entire town bringing up the past and ganging up on him. "Shelly and I have business to discuss, if none of you mind."

Allen Davis, who had worked with Dare's grandfather years ago, crossed his arms over his chest. "Considering what you did to her, yes, we do mind. So you better behave yourself where she is concerned, Dare Westmoreland. Don't forget there's an election next year."

Dare had just about had it, and was about to tell Mr. Davis a thing or two when Shelly piped in, laughing. "I can't believe all of you still remember what happened ten years ago. I'd almost forgotten about that," she lied. "And to this day I still consider Dare my good friend," she lied again, and tried tactfully to change the subject. "Ms. Mamie, how is Mr. Fred?"

"He still can't hear worth a dime, but other than that he's fine. Thanks for asking. Now to get back to the subject of Dare here, from the way he used to sniff behind you and kept all the other boys away from you, we all thought he was going to be your husband," Mamie mumbled, glaring at Dare.

Shelly shook her head, seeing that the older woman was determined to have her say. She placed a hand on Ms. Mamie's arm in a warm display of affection. "Yes, I know you all did and that was sweet. But things didn't work out that way and we can't worry about spilled milk now can we?"

Ms. Mamie smiled up at Shelly and patted her hand. "I guess not, dear, but watch yourself around him. I know how crazy you were about him before. There's no need for a woman to let the same man break her heart twice."

Dare frowned, not appreciating Mamie Potter talking about him as if he wasn't there. Nor did it help matters that Shelly was looking at him as though she'd just been given good sound advice. He cleared his throat, thinking that it was time he broke up the little gathering. He placed his hand on Shelly's arm and said. "This way, Shelly. We need to discuss our business so I can get to the office. We can talk now or you can join Jared and I for lunch."

From the look on her face he could tell his words had reminded her of why he was meeting Jared for lunch. After telling everyone goodbye and giving out a few more hugs, she turned and followed Dare to a booth, the farthest one in the back.

He stood aside while she slipped into a soft padded seat and then he slid into the one across from her. Nervously she traced the floral designs on the placemat. Dare's nearness was getting to her. She had experienced the same thing in his office last night, and it aggravated the heck out of her that all that anger she'd felt for him had not been able to diffuse her desire for him; especially after ten years.

Desire.

That had to be what it was since she knew she was no longer in love with him. He had effectively put an end to those feelings years ago. Yet, for some reason she was feeling the same turbulent yearnings she'd always felt for him. And last night in her bed, the memories had been at their worse…or their best, depending on how you looked at it.

She had awakened in the middle of the night with her breath coming in deep, ragged gasps, and her sheets damp with perspiration after a hot, steamy dream about him.

Getting up and drinking a glass of ice water, she had made a decision not to beat herself up over her dreams of Dare. She'd decided that the reason for them was understandable. Her body knew Dare as it knew no other man, and it had reminded her of that fact in a not-too-subtle way. It didn't help that for the past ten years she hadn't dated much; raising AJ and working at the hospital kept her busy, and the few occasions she had dated had been a complete waste of her time since she'd never experienced the sparks with any of them that she'd grown accustomed to with Dare.

"Would you like some more coffee, Sheriff?"

Shelly snatched her head up when she heard the sultry, feminine voice and was just in time to see the slow smile that spread across the young woman's lips, as well as the look of wanton hunger in her eyes as she looked at Dare. Either he didn't notice or he was doing a pretty good job of pretending not to.

"Yes, Lizzie, I'd like another cup."

"And what would you like?" Lizzie asked her, and Shelly couldn't help but notice the cold, unfriendly eyes that were staring at her.

Evidently the same thing you would like, Shelly thought, trying to downplay the envy she suddenly felt, although she knew there was no legitimate reason to feel that way. What was once between her and Dare had ended years ago and she didn't intend to go back there, no matter how much he could still arouse her. Sighing, she was about to give the woman her order when Dare spoke. "She would like a cup of coffee with cream and one sugar."

The waitress lifted her brow as if wondering how Dare knew what Shelly wanted. "Okay, Sheriff." Lizzie placed menus in front of them, saying, "I'll bring your coffee while you take a look at these."

When Lizzie had left, Shelly leaned in closer to the center of the booth and whispered, "I don't appreciate the daggered looks coming from one of your girlfriends." She decided not to tell him that she'd felt like throwing a few daggered looks of her own.

Lifting his head from the menu, Dare frowned. "What are you talking about? I've never dated Lizzie. She's just a kid."

Shelly shrugged as she straightened in her seat and glanced over to where Lizzie was now taking another order. Her short uniform showed off quite nicely the curves of her body and her long legs. Dare was wrong. Lizzie was no kid. Her body attested to that.

"Well, kid or no kid, she definitely has the hots for you, Dare Westmoreland."

He shrugged. "You're imagining things."

"No, trust me. I know."

He rubbed his chin as his mouth tipped up crookedly into a smile. Settling back in his seat, he asked, "And how would you know?"

She met his gaze. "Because I'm a woman." And I know all about having the hots for you, she decided not to add.

Dare nodded. He definitely couldn't deny that she was a woman. He glanced over at Lizzie and caught her at the exact moment she was looking at him with a flirty smile. He remembered the other times she'd given him that smile, and now it all made sense. He quickly averted his eyes. Clearing his throat, he met Shelly's gaze. "I've never noticed before."

Typical man, Shelly thought, but before she could say anything else, Lizzie had returned with their coffee. After taking their order she left, and Shelly smiled and said, "I can't believe you remembered how I like my coffee after all this time."

Dare looked at her. His gaze remained steady when he said. "There are some things a man can't forget about a woman he considered as his, Shelly."

"Oh," her voice was slightly shaky, and she decided not to touch that one; mainly because what he said was true. He had considered her as his; she had been his in every way a woman could belong to a man.

She took a deep breath before taking a sip of coffee. Emotions she didn't want to feel were churning inside her. Dare had hurt her once and she refused to let him do so again. She would definitely take Ms. Mamie's advice and watch herself around him. She glanced up and noticed Dare watching her. The heat from his gaze made her feel a connection to him, one she didn't want to feel, but she realized they did have a connection.

Their son.

She cleared her throat, deciding they needed to engage in conversation, something she considered a safe topic. "How is your family doing?"

A warm smile appeared on Dare's face. "Mom and Dad and all the rest of the Westmoreland clan are fine."

Shelly took another sip of her coffee then asked. "Is it true what I've heard about Delaney? Did she actually finish medical school and marry a sheikh?" she asked. She wondered how that had happened when everyone knew how overprotective the Westmoreland brothers had been of their baby sister.

Dare smiled and the heat in his gaze eased somewhat. "Yeah, it's true. The one and only time we took our eyes off Laney, she slipped away and hid out in a cabin in the mountains for a little rest and relaxation. While there she met this sheikh from the Middle East. Their marriage took some getting used to, since she up and moved to his country. They have a five-month-old son named Ari."

"Have you seen him yet?"

Dare's smile widened. "Yes, the entire family was there for his birth and it was some sort of experience." A frown appeared on his face when he suddenly thought about what he'd missed out on by not being there when AJ had come into the world. "Tell me about AJ, Shelly. Tell me how things were when he was born."

Shelly swallowed thickly. So much for thinking she had moved to a safe topic of conversation. She sighed, knowing Dare had a right to what he was asking for. "He was born in the hospital where I worked. My parents were there with me. I didn't gain much weight while pregnant and that helped make the delivery easier. He wasn't a big baby, only a little over six pounds, but he was extremely long which accounts for his height. As soon as I saw him I immediately thought he looked like you. And I knew at that moment no matter how we had separated, that my baby was a part of you."

Shelly hesitated for a few moments and added. "That's why I gave him your name, Dare. In my mind he didn't look like a Marcus, which was the name I had intended to give him. To me he looked like an Alisdare Julian. A little Dare."

Dare didn't say anything for the longest time, then he said. "Thank you for doing that."

"You're welcome."

Moments later, Dare cleared his throat and asked. "Does he know he was named after his father?"

"Yes. You don't know how worried I was before arriving at the police station yesterday. I was afraid that you had found out his name, or that he had found out yours. Luckily for me, most people at the station call you Sheriff, and everyone in town still calls you Dare."

Dare nodded. "Except for my family, few people probably remember my real name is Alisdare since it's seldom used. I've always gone by Dare. If AJ had given me his full name I would have figured things out."

After a few brief quiet moments, Dare said. "I told my parents and my brothers about him last night, Shelly."

She nervously bit into her bottom lip. "And what were their reactions?"

Dare leaned back against his seat and met her gaze. "They were as shocked as I was, and of course they're anxious to meet him."

Shelly nodded slowly. She'd figured they would be. The Westmorelands were a big family and a rather close-knit group. "Dare, about your suggestion on how we should handle things."

"Yes?"

She didn't say anything for the longest time, then she said. "I'll go along with your plan as long as you and I understand something."

"What?"

"That it will be strictly for show. There's no way the two of us could ever get back together for any reason. The only thing between us is AJ."

Dare raised a brow and gave her a deliberate look. He wondered why she was so damn sure of that, but decided to let it go for now. He wanted to start building a relationship with his son immediately, and he refused to let Shelly put stumbling blocks in his way. "That's fine with me."

He leaned back in his chair. "So how soon will you tell AJ about me?"

"I plan to tell him tonight."

Dare nodded, satisfied with her answer. That meant they could put their plans into action as early as tomorrow. "I think we're doing the right thing, Shelly."

She felt the intensity of his gaze, and the force of it touched her in a way she didn't want. "I hope so, Dare. I truly hope so," she said quietly.

Four

Dare glanced at the clock again and sighed deeply. Where was AJ? School had let out over an hour ago and he still hadn't arrived. According to what Shelly had told him that morning at breakfast, AJ had ridden his bike to school and been told to report to the sheriff's office as soon as school was out. Dare wondered if AJ had blatantly disobeyed his mother.

Although Shelly had given him her cell-phone number—as a home healthcare nurse she would be making various house calls today—he didn't want to call and get her worried or upset. If he had to, he would go looking for their son himself and when he found him, he intended to—"

The sound of the buzzer interrupted his thoughts. "Yes, McKade, what is it?"

"That Brockman kid is here."

Dare nodded and sighed with relief. Then he recalled what McKade had said—*that Brockman kid*. He frowned.

The first thing he planned to do when everything settled was to give his son his last name. *That Westmoreland kid* sounded more to his liking. "Okay, I'll be right out."

Leaving his office, Dare walked down the hall toward the front of the building and stopped dead in his tracks when he saw AJ. His frown deepened. The kid looked as though he'd had a day with a tiger. "What happened to you?" he asked him, his gaze roaming over AJ's torn shirt and soiled jeans, not to mention his bruised lip and blood-ied nose.

"Nothing happened. I fell off my bike," AJ snapped.

Dare glanced over at McKade. They both recognized a lie when they heard one. Dare crossed his arms over his chest. "You never came across to me as the outright clumsy type."

That got the response Dare was hoping for. The anger flaring in AJ's eyes deepened. "I am not the clumsy type. Anyone can fall off a bike," he said, again snapping out his answer.

"Yes, but in this case that's not what happened and you know it," Dare said, wanting to snap back but didn't. It was apparent that AJ had been in a fight, and Dare decided to cut the crap. "Tell me what really happened."

"I'm not telling you anything."

Wrong answer, Dare thought taking a step forward to stand in front of AJ. "Look, kid, we can stand here all day until you decide to talk, but you *will* tell me what happened."

AJ stuck his hands in the pockets of his jeans and glanced down as if to study the expensive pair of Air Jor-dans on his feet. When seconds ticked into minutes and he saw that Dare would not move an inch, he finally raised his head, met Dare's gaze, squared his shoulders and said. "Caleb Martin doesn't like me and today after school he decided to take his dislike to another level."

Dare leaned against the counter and raised a brow. "And?"

AJ paused, squared his shoulders again and said. "And I decided to oblige him. He pushed me down and when I got up I made sure he found out the hard way that I'm not someone to mess with."

Dare inwardly smiled. He hated admitting it but what his son had said had been spoken like a true Westmoreland. He didn't want to remember the number of times one of the Westmoreland boys came home with something bloodied or broken. Word had soon gotten around school that those Westmorelands weren't anyone to tangle with. They never went looking for trouble, but they knew how to handle it when it came their way.

"Fighting doesn't accomplish anything."

His son shrugged. "Maybe not, but I bet Caleb Martin won't be calling me bad names and pushing me around again. I had put up with it long enough.

Dare placed his hand on his hips. "If this has been going on for a while, why didn't you say something about it to your mother or to some adult at school?"

AJ's glare deepened even more. "I'm not a baby. I don't need my mother or some teacher fighting my battles for me."

Dare met his son's glare with one of his own. "Maybe not, but in the future I expect you not to take matters into your own hands. If I hear about it, I will haul both you and that Martin kid in here and the two of you will be sorry. Not only will I assign after-school duties but I'll give weekend work duties as well. I won't tolerate that kind of foolishness." Especially when it involved his son, Dare decided not to add. "Now go into that bathroom and get cleaned up then meet me out back."

AJ shifted his book bag to his other shoulder. "What am I supposed to do today?"

"My police car needs washing and I can use the help."

AJ nodded and rushed off toward the bathroom. Dare couldn't hide the smile that lit his face. Although AJ had grumbled last night about having to show up at the police station after school, Dare could tell from his expression that he enjoyed having something to do.

"Sheriff?"

Dare glanced up and met McKade's gaze. "Yes?"

"There's something about that kid that's oddly familiar."

Dare knew what McKade was getting at. His deputy had seen the paperwork he'd completed last night and had probably put two and two together; especially since Rick McKade knew his first and middle names. The two of them were good friends and had been since joining the FBI at the same time years back. When Dare had decided to leave the Bureau, so had McKade. Rick had followed Dare to Atlanta, where he'd met and fallen in love with a school-teacher who lived in the area.

"The reason he seems oddly familiar, McKade, is because you just saw him yesterday," Dare said, hoping that was the end of it.

He found out it wasn't when McKade chuckled and said. "That's not what I mean and you know it, Dare. There's something else."

"What?"

McKade paused a moment before answering. "He looks a lot like you and your brothers, but *especially* like you." He again paused a few moments then asked. "Is there anything you want to tell me?"

Dare's lips curved into a smile. He didn't have to tell McKade anything since it was obvious he had figured things out for himself. "No, there's nothing I want to tell you."

McKade chuckled again. "Then maybe I better tell you, or rather I should remind you that the people in this town don't know how to keep a secret if that's what you plan to do. It won't be long before everyone figures things out, and when they do, someone will tell the kid."

Dare's smile widened when he thought of that happening. "Yes, and that's what his mother and I are counting on." Knowing what he'd said had probably confused the hell out of McKade, Dare turned and walked through the door that led out back.

The kid was a hard worker and a darn good one at that, Dare decided as he watched AJ dry off the police cruiser. He had only intended the job to last an hour, but he could tell that AJ was actually enjoying having something to do. He made a mental note to ask Shelly if AJ did any chores at home, and if not, maybe it wouldn't be a bad idea for her to assign him a few. That would be another way to keep him out of trouble.

"Is this it for the day?"

AJ's statement jerked Dare from his thoughts. AJ had placed the cloth he'd used to dry off the car back in the bucket. "Yes, that's it, but make sure you come back tomorrow—and I expect you to be on time."

A scowl appeared on AJ's face but he didn't say anything as he picked up his book bag and placed it on his shoulder. "I don't like coming here after school."

Dare shook his head and inwardly smiled, wondering who the kid was trying to convince. "Well, you should have thought of that before you got into trouble."

Their gazes locked for a brief moment and Dare detected a storm of defiance brewing within his son. "How much longer do I have to come here?" AJ asked in an agitated voice.

"Until I think you've learned your lesson."

AJ's glare deepened. "Well, I don't like it."

Dare raised his gaze upward to the sky then looked back

to AJ. "You've said that already kid, but in this case what you like doesn't really matter. When you break the law you have to be punished. That's something I suggest you remember. I also suggest that you get home before your mother starts worrying about you," he said, following AJ inside the building.

"She's going to do that anyway."

Dare smiled. "Yeah, I wouldn't put it past her, since mothers are that way. I'm sure my four brothers and I worried my mother a lot when we were growing up."

AJ raised a brow. "You have four brothers?"

Dare's smile widened. "Yes, I have four brothers and one sister. I'm the oldest of the group.

AJ nodded. "It's just me and my mom."

Dare nodded as well. He then stood in front of the door with A. J. "To answer your question of how long you'll have to come here after school, I think a full week of this should make you think twice about throwing rocks at passing cars the next time." Dare rubbed his chin thoughtfully then added. "Unless I hear about you getting involved in a fight again. Like I said, that's something I won't tolerate."

AJ glared at him. "Then I'll make sure you don't hear about it."

Not giving Dare a chance to respond, AJ raced out of the door, got his bike and took off.

"Ouch, that hurts!"

"Well, this should teach you a lesson," Shelly said angrily, leaning over AJ as she applied antiseptic to his bruised lip. "And if I hear of you fighting again, I will put you on a punishment like you wouldn't believe."

"He started it!"

Shelly straightened and met her son's dark scowl. "Then next time walk away," she said firmly.

"People are going to think I'm a coward if I do that. I told you I was going to hate it here. Nobody likes me. At least I had friends in L.A."

"I don't consider those guys you hung around with back in L.A. your friends. A true friend wouldn't talk you into doing bad things, AJ, and as far as anyone thinking you're a coward, then let them. I know for a fact that you're one of the bravest persons I know. Look how long you've had to be the man of the house for me."

AJ shrugged and glanced up at his mother. "But it's different with you, Mom. I don't want any of the guys at school thinking I'm a pushover."

"Trust me, you're not a pushover. You're too much like your father." She then turned to walk toward the kitchen.

Shelly knew she had thrown out the hook and it wouldn't take long for AJ to take the bait. She heard him draw in a long breath behind her and knew he was right on her heels.

"Why did you mention him?"

She looked back over her shoulder at AJ when she reached the kitchen. "Why did I mention who?"

"My father."

She leaned against the kitchen cabinet and raised a curious brow. "I'm not supposed to mention him?"

"You haven't in a long time."

Shelly nodded. "Only because you haven't asked about him in a long time. Tonight when you said something about being a pushover, I immediately thought of him because you're so much like him and he's one of the bravest men I know."

AJ smiled. He was glad to know his father was brave. "What does he do, fly planes or something?"

Shelly smiled knowing of her son's fixation with airplanes and spaceships. "No." She inhaled deeply. "I think it's time we had a talk about your father. I've been doing a lot of thinking since moving back and I need you to help me make a decision about something."

AJ lifted a brow. "A decision about what?"

"About whether to tell your father about you."

Surprised widened AJ's eyes. "You know where he is?"

Shelly shook her head. "AJ, I've always known where he is. I've always told you that. And I've always told you if you ever wanted me to contact him to just say the word."

Uncertainty narrowed his eyes, then he glanced down as if to study his sneakers. "Yeah, but I wasn't sure if you really meant it or not," he said quietly.

Shelly smiled weakly and reached out and gently gripped his chin to bring his gaze back to hers. "Is that why you stopped asking me about him? You thought I was lying to you about him?"

He shrugged. "I just figured you were saying what you wanted me to believe. Nick Banner's mom did that to him. She told him that his dad had died in a car accident when he was a baby, then one day he heard his grandpa tell somebody that his dad was alive and had another family someplace and that he didn't want Nick."

Shelly's breath caught in her throat. She felt an urgent need to take her son into her arms and assure him that unlike Nick's father, his father did want him. But she knew he was now at an age where mothers' hugs were no longer *cool*. Her heart felt heavy knowing that AJ had denied himself knowledge of his father in an attempt to save her from what he thought was embarrassment.

"Come on, let's sit at the table. I think it's time for us to have a long talk."

AJ hung his head thoughtfully then glanced back at her. His eyes were wary. "About him?"

"Yes about him. There are things I think you need to know, so come on."

He followed her over to the table and they sat down. Her gaze was steady as she met his. "Now then, just to set the record straight, everything I've ever told you about your father was true. He was someone I dated through high school and college while I lived here in College Park. Everyone in town thought we would marry, and I guess that had been my thought too, but your father had a dream."

"A dream?"

"Yes, a dream of one day becoming an FBI agent. You have your dream to grow up and become an astronaut one day don't you?"

"Yes."

"Well, your father had a similar dream, but his was one day to become an FBI agent, and I knew if I had told him that I was pregnant with you, he would have turned his back on his dream for us. I didn't want him to do that. I loved him too much. So, without telling him I was pregnant with you, I left town. So he never knew about you, AJ."

Shelly sighed. Everything she'd just told AJ was basically true. However, this next part would be a lie; a lie Dare was convinced AJ needed to believe. "Your father still doesn't know about you, and this is where I need your help."

AJ looked confused. "My help about what?"

"About what I should do." When his confusion didn't clear she said, "Since we moved back, I found out your father is still living here in College Park."

She could tell AJ was momentarily taken aback by what she'd said. He stared at her with wide, expressive eyes. "He's here? In this town?" he asked in a somewhat shaky yet excited voice.

"Yes. It seems that he moved back a few years ago after he stopped working for the FBI in Washington, D.C." Shelly leaned back in her chair. "I want to be fair to the both of you. You're getting older and so is he. I think it's time that I finally tell him about you, just like I'm telling you about him."

AJ nodded and looked her and she saw uncertainty in his eyes. "But what if he doesn't want me?"

Shelly smiled and then chuckled. "Trust me, when he finds out about you he will definitely want you. In fact I'm a little concerned about what his reaction will be when he realizes that I've kept your existence from him. He is a man who strongly believes in family and he won't be a happy camper."

"Had he known about me, he would have married you?"

Shelly's smiled widened, knowing that was true. "Yes, in a heartbeat, which is the reason I didn't tell him. And although it's too late for either of us to think of ever having a life together again, because we've lived separate lives for so long, there's no doubt in my mind that once I tell him about you he'll want to become a part of your life. But I need to know how you feel about that."

AJ shrugged. "I'm okay with it, but how do you feel about it. Mom?"

"I'm okay with it, too."

AJ nodded. He then lowered his head as his finger made designs across the tablecloth. Moments later he lifted his eyes and met her gaze. "So when can I get to meet him?"

Shelly took a deep breath and hoped that her next words sounded normal. "You've already met your father, AJ. You met him yesterday."

She inhaled deeply then broke it down further by saying, "Sheriff Dare Westmoreland is your father."

Five

"Sheriff Westmoreland!" AJ shouted as he jumped out of his seat. He stood in front of his mother and lifted his chin angrily, defiantly. "It can't be him. No way."

Shelly smiled slightly. "Trust me, it *is* him. I of all people should know."

"But—but, I don't want *him* to be my father," he huffed loudly.

Shelly looked directly at AJ, at how badly he was taking the news, which really wasn't unexpected, considering the way he and Dare had clashed. "I'm sorry you feel that way because he is and there's nothing you can do about it. Alisdare Julian Westmoreland *is* your father."

When she saw the look that crossed his face, she added. "And I didn't make up that part either. You really were named after him, AJ. He merely shortens the Alisdare to Dare."

She felt AJ's need to deny what she'd just told him, but there was no way she could let him do that. "The question is, now that you know he's your father, what are we going to do about it?"

She watched his forehead scrunch into a frown, then he said. "We don't have to do anything about it since he doesn't have to know. We can continue with things the way they are."

She lifted a brow. "Don't you think he has every right to know about you?"

"Not if I don't want him to know."

Shelly shook her head. "Dare will be very hurt if he ever learns the truth." She studied her son. "Can you give me a good reason why he shouldn't be told?"

"Yes, because he doesn't like me and I don't like him."

Shelly met his gaze. "With your disrespectful attitude, you probably didn't make a good impression on him yesterday, AJ. However, Dare loves kids. And as far as you not liking him, you really don't know him, and I think you should get to know him. He's really a nice guy, otherwise I would not have fallen in love with him all those years ago." A small voice whispered that that part was true. Dare had always been a caring and loving person. "How did things go between the two of you today?"

AJ shrugged. "We still don't like each other, and I don't want to get to know him. So please don't tell him, Mom. You can't."

She paused for a moment knowing what she would say, knowing she would not press him anymore. "All right, AJ, since you feel so strongly about it, I won't tell him. But I'm hoping that one day *you* will be the one to tell him. I'm hoping that one day you'll see the importance of him knowing the truth."

She stood and walked over to AJ and placed her hand on his shoulder. "There's something else you need to think about."

"What?"

"Dare is a very smart man. Chances are he'll figure things out without either one of us telling him anything."

He frowned and his eyes grew round. "How?"

Shelly smiled. "You favor him and his four brothers. Although he hasn't noticed it yet, there's a good chance that he will. And then there's the question of your age. He knows I left town ten years ago, the same year you were born."

AJ nodded. "Did he ask you anything when you saw him yesterday?"

"No. I think he assumes your father is someone I met after leaving here, but as I said, there's a chance he might start putting two and two together."

AJ's features drew in a deeper frown at the thought of that happening. "But we can't let him figure it out."

She shook her head. Shelly hated lying to AJ although she knew it was for a good reason. She had to remember that. "Whoa. Don't include me in this, AJ. It's strictly your decision not to let Dare know about you, it isn't mine. I'm already in hot water for not having told him that you exist at all. But I'll keep my word and not tell him anything if that's the way you want it."

"Yes, that's the way I want it," AJ said, not hiding the relief on his face.

His lips were quivering, and Shelly knew he was fighting hard to keep his tears at bay. Right now he was feeling torn. A part of him wanted to be elated that his father did exist, but another part refused to accept the man who he'd discovered his father was, all because of that Westmoreland pride and stubbornness.

Shelly shook her head when she felt tears in the back of her own eyes. Dare's mission to win his son's love would not be easy.

Later that night, after AJ had gone to bed Shelly received a phone call from Dare.

"Did you tell him?"

She leaned against her kitchen sink. "Yes, I told him."

There was a pause. "And how did he take it?"

Shelly released a deep sigh. "Just as we expected. He doesn't want you to know that he's your son." When Dare didn't respond, she said. "Don't take it personally, Dare. I think he's more confused than anything right now. Tonight I discovered why he had stopped asking me about you."

"Why?"

"Because he didn't really believe you existed, at least not the way I'd told him. It seems that a friend of his had shared with him the fact that his mother had told him his father had died in a car accident when he was a baby, and then he'd discovered that his father was alive and well and living somewhere with another family. So AJ assumed what I had told him about you wasn't true and that I really didn't know how to contact you if he ever asked me to. And since he never wanted to place me in a position that showed me up as a liar, he just never bothered."

Again she released a sigh as she fought back the tears that threaten to fall. "And to think that he probably did want to know you all this time but refrained from asking to save me embarrassment in being caught in a lie."

A sob caught in her throat as she blinked back a tear. "Oh, Dare I feel so bad for him, and what he's going through is all my fault. I thought I was making all the right decisions for all the right reasons and now it seems I caused more harm than good."

Dare lay in bed, his entire body tense. He could no longer hold back the anger he felt for Shelly, even knowing he had made a couple of mistakes himself in handling things ten years ago. Had he not chosen a career over her then, things would have worked out a whole lot differently. So, in reality, he was just as much to blame as Shelly, but together they had a chance to make things work to save their son.

"Things are going to work out in the end, Shell, you'll see. You've done your part tonight, now let me handle things from here. It might take months, but in the end I believe that AJ will accept me as his father. In my heart I believe that one day he'll want me to know the truth."

Shelly nodded, hearing the confidence in Dare's voice and hoping he was right. "So now we move to the second phase of your plan?"

"Now we move to the second phase of *our* plan."

The next morning, after AJ had left for school, a gentle knock on the door alerted Shelly that she had a visitor. Today was her day off and she had spent the last half hour or so on the computer paying her bills on-line, and was just about to walk into the kitchen for a cup of coffee.

Crossing the living room she glanced out of the peephole. Her breath caught. Dare was standing on her porch, and his tall, muscular frame was silhouetted by the mid-morning sunlight that was shining brightly behind him. He looked gorgeous; his uniform, which showcased his solid chest, firm stomach and strong flanks, made him look even more so.

She shivered as everything about her that was woman jolted upward from the soles of her feet, to settle in an area between her legs. She inhaled and commanded her body not to go there. Whatever had been between her and Dare had ended ten years ago, and now was not the time for her body to go horny on her. She'd done without sex for this long, and she could continue to go without it for a while longer. But damn if Dare Westmoreland didn't rattle and stir up those urges she'd kept dormant for ten years. She couldn't for the life of her forget how it had felt to run her hands over his chest, indulging in the crisp feel of his chair and the masculine texture of his skin.

She closed her eyes and took a deep breath at the memory of his firm stomach rubbing against her own and the feel of his calloused palm touching her intimately on the sensitive areas of her body. She remembered him awakening within her a passion that had almost startled her.

His second knock made her regain her mental balance, and warning signals against opening the door suddenly went off in her head as she opened her eyes. A silent voice reminded her that although she might want to, there was no way to put as much distance between herself and Dare as she'd like. No matter how much being around him got to her, their main concern was their son.

Inhaling deeply, she slowly opened the door and met his gaze. Once again she felt every sexual instinct she possessed spring to life. "Dare, what are you doing here?" she asked, pausing afterwards to take a deep, steadying breath.

He smiled, that enticingly sexy smile that always made her want to go to the nearest bed and get it on with him. There was no way she couldn't see him and not think of crawling into bed next to him amidst rumpled sheets while he reached out and took her into his arms and…

"I tried calling you at the agency where you worked and they told me you were off today," he said as he leaned in her doorway, breaking into her wayward thoughts and sending her already sex-crazed mind into turmoil. Why did he still look so good after ten years? And why on earth was her body responding to the sheer essence of him this way? But then she and Dare always had had an abundant amount of overzealous hormones and it seemed that ten years hadn't done a thing to change that.

"Why were you trying to reach me?" she somehow found her voice to ask him. "Is something wrong?"

He shook his head, immediately putting her fears to rest. "No, but I thought it would be a good idea if we talked."

Shelly's eyebrows raised. "Talk? But we talked yesterday morning at Kate's Diner and again last night. What do we have to talk about now?" she asked, trying not to sound as frustrated as she felt.

"I thought you'd like to know how my meeting went with Jared yesterday."

"Oh." She had completely forgotten about his plans to meet with his attorney cousin for lunch. She'd always liked his cousin Jared Westmoreland, who, over the years, had become something of a hotshot attorney. "I would." She took a step back as she fought to remain composed. "Come in."

He stepped inside and closed the door behind him and then glanced around. "It's been years since I've been inside this house. It brings back memories," Dare said meeting her gaze once again.

She nodded, remembering how he used to stand in that same spot countless times as he waited for her to come down the stairs for their dates. And even then, when she breezed down the stairs her mind was filled with thoughts of their evening, especially how it would finish. "Yes, it does."

A long, seemingly endless moment of silence stretched between them before she finally cleared her throat. "I was about to have a cup of coffee and a Danish if you'd like to join me," she offered.

"That's a pretty tempting offer, one that I think I'll take you up on."

Shelly nodded. If he thought *that* was tempting he really didn't know what tempting was about. *Tempting* was Dare Westmoreland standing in the middle of her living room looking absolutely gorgeous. And it didn't help matters one iota when she glanced his way and saw a definite bulge behind his fly. Apparently he was just as hot and bothered as she was.

She quickly turned around. "Follow me," she said over her shoulder, wondering how she was going to handle being alone in the house with him.

Following Shelly was the last thing Dare thought he needed to do. He tried not to focus on the sway of the backside encased in denim shorts in front of him. He was suddenly besieged with memories of just how that backside had felt in his hands when he'd lifted it to thrust inside her. Those thoughts made his arousal harden even more. He suppressed a groan deep in his throat.

He tried to think of other things and glanced around. He liked the way she had decorated the place, totally differently from the way her parents used to have it. Her mother's taste had been soft and quaint. Shelly's taste made a bold statement. She liked colors—bright cheery colors—evident in the vivid print of the sofa, loveseat and wingback chair. Then there were her walls, painted in a variety of colorful shades, so different from his plain off-white ones. He was amazed how she was able to tie everything together without anything clashing. She had managed to create a cozy and homey atmosphere for herself and AJ.

As they entered the kitchen, Dare quickly sat down at the table before she could note the fix his body was in, if she hadn't done so already. But he soon discovered that sitting at the table watching her move around the kitchen only intensified his problem. He was getting even more turned on by the fluid movements of her body as she reached into a cabinet to get their coffee cups. The shorts were snug, a perfect fit, and his entire body began throbbing in deep male appreciation.

"You still like your coffee black and your Danish with a lot of butter, Dare?"

"Yes," he managed to respond. He began to realize that he had made a mistake in dropping by. Over the past couple of days when they'd been together there had been other people around. Now it was just the two of them, alone in this house, in this room. He had to fight hard to dismiss the thought of taking her right there on the table.

He inhaled deeply. If Shelly knew what thoughts were running through his mind she would probably hightail it up the stairs, which wouldn't do her any good since he would only race up those same stairs after her and end up making love to her in one of the bedrooms.

That was something they had done once before when her parents had been out of town and he had dropped by unexpectedly. A slow, lazy smile touched the side of his mouth as he remembered the intensity of their lovemaking that day. That was the one time they hadn't used protection. Perhaps that was the time she had gotten pregnant with AJ?

"What are you smiling about?"

Her question invaded his thoughts and he shifted in the chair to alleviate some of the tension pressing at the zipper of his pants. He met her gaze and decided to be completely honest with her, something he had always done. "I was thinking about that time that we made love upstairs in your bedroom without protection, and wondered if that was the time you got pregnant."

"It was."

He regarded her for a second. "How do you know?"

She stared at the floor for a moment before meeting his gaze again. "Because after that was the first time I'd ever been late."

He nodded. The reason they had made love so recklessly

and intensely that day was because he had received orders a few hours earlier to leave immediately for an area near Kuwait. It was a temporary assignment and he would only be gone for two months. But at the time, two months could have been two years for all she cared. Because of the danger of his assignment, the news had immediately sent her in a spin and she had raced up the stairs to her bedroom so he wouldn't see her cry. He had gone after her, only to end up placing her on the bed and making frantic, uncontrolled love to her.

"What did Jared have to say yesterday?" Shelly asked him rather than think about that particular day when they had unknowingly created their son. Straightening, she walked over to the table and placed the coffee and rolls in front of him, then sat down at the table.

He took a sip of coffee and responded, "Jared thinks that whatever we decide is the best way to handle letting AJ know I'm his father is fine as long as we're in agreement. But he strongly thinks I should do whatever needs to be done to compensate you from the time he was born. And I agree. As his father I had certain responsibilities to him."

"But you didn't know about him, Dare."

"But I know about him now, Shelly, and that makes a world of difference."

Shelly nodded. She knew that to argue with Dare would be a complete waste of her time. "All right, I have a college fund set up and if you'd like to contribute, I have no problem with that. That is definitely one way you can help."

Dare leaned back in his chair and met her gaze. "Are you sure there's no other way I can help?"

For a moment she wondered if he was asking for AJ or for her. Could he detect the deep longing within her, the sexual cravings, and knew he could help her there? She sighed, knowing she was letting her mind become cluttered. AJ was the only thing between them, and she had to remember that.

"Yes, I'm sure," she said softly. "My job pays well and I've always budgeted to live within my means. The cost of living isn't as high here as it is in L.A., and my parents aren't charging me any rent, so AJ and I are fine, Dare, but thanks for asking."

At that moment the telephone rang; she hoped he didn't see the relief on her face. "Excuse me," she said, standing quickly. "That's probably the agency calling to let me know my hours and clients for next week."

As Shelly listened to the agency's secretary tell her what her schedule would be for the following week, she tried to get her thoughts back together. Dare had stirred up emotions and needs that she'd thought were dead and buried until she'd seen him two days ago. His presence had blood racing through her body at an alarming speed.

"All right, thanks for calling," she said before hanging up the phone. She quickly turned and bumped into a massive solid chest. "Oh."

Dare reached out and quickly stopped Shelly from falling. "Sorry, I didn't mean to scare you," he said, his words soft and gentle.

She took a step back when he released her. Each time he touched her she was reminded of the sensual feelings he could easily invoke. "I thought you were still sitting down."

"I thought it was time for me to leave. I don't want to take you from your work any longer."

She rubbed her hands across her arms, knowing it was best if he left. "Is that all Jared said?"

He nodded. That was all she needed to know. There was no need to tell her that Jared had suggested the possibility of him having legal visitation rights and petitioning for joint custody of AJ. Both suggestions he had squashed, since he and Shelly had devised what they considered a workable plan.

His gaze moved to her hands and he watched her fingers sliding back and forth across her arms. He remembered her doing that very thing on a certain part of his anatomy several times. The memory of the warmth of her fingers touching him so intimately slammed another arousal through his body that strengthened the one already there.

At that moment, he lost whatever control he had. Being around her stirred up memories and emotions he could no longer fight, nor did he want to. The only thing he wanted, he needed, was to kiss her, taste her and reacquaint the insides of his mouth, his tongue, with hers.

Shelly was having issues of her own and took a steadying breath, trying to get the heated desire racing through her body under control. She swallowed deeply when she saw that Dare's gaze was dead-centered on her mouth, and fought off the panic that seized her when he took a step forward.

"I wonder…" he said huskily, his gaze not leaving her lips.

She blinked, refocused on him. "You wonder about what?" she asked softly, feeling the last shreds of her composure slipping.

"I wonder if your mouth still knows me."

His words cut through any control she had left. Those were the words he had always whispered whenever they were together after being apart for any length of time, just moments before he took her into his arms and kissed her senseless.

He leaned in closer, then lowered his mouth to hers. Immediately, his tongue went after hers in an attempt to lure her into the same rush of desire consuming him. But she was already there, a step ahead of him, so he tried forcing his body to calm down and settle into the taste he'd always been accustomed to. He had expected heat, but he hadn't expected the hot, fiery explosion that went off in his mid-section. It made a groan erupt from deep in his throat.

His hands linked around her waist to hold her closer, thigh-to-thigh, breasts to chest. Sensation after sensation speared through him, making it hard to resist eating her alive, or at least trying to, and wanting to touch her everywhere, especially between her legs. Now that he had rediscovered this—the taste of her mouth—he wanted also to relive the feel of his fingers sliding over her heated flesh to find the hot core of her, swollen and wet.

That thought drove a primitive need through him and the erection pressing against her got longer and harder. The thought of using it to penetrate the very core of her made his mind reel and drugged his brain even more with her sensuality.

A shiver raced over Shelly and a semblance of control returned as she realized just how easily she had succumbed to his touch. She knew she had to put a halt to what they were doing. She had returned to College Park not for herself but for AJ.

She broke off their kiss and untangled herself from his arms. When he leaned toward her, to kiss her again, she pushed him back. "No, Dare," she said firmly. "We shouldn't have done that. This isn't about you or me or our inability to control overzealous hormones. It's about our son and doing what is best for him."

And why can't we simultaneously discover what is best for us, he wanted to ask but refrained from doing so. He understood her need to put AJ first and foremost, but what she would soon realize was that there was unfinished business between them as well. "I agree that AJ is our main concern, Shelly, but there's something you need to realize and accept."

"What?"

"Things aren't over between us, and we shouldn't deceive ourselves into thinking there won't be a next time, so be prepared for it."

He saw the frown that appeared in her eyes and the defiance that tilted her lips reminded him of AJ yesterday and the day before. "No, Dare, there won't be a next time because I won't let there be. You're AJ's father, but what was between us is over and has been for years. To me you're just another man."

He lifted a brow. He wondered if she had kissed many men the way she'd kissed him, and for some reason he doubted it. She had kissed him as though she hadn't kissed anyone in years. He had felt the hunger that had raged through her. He had felt it, explored it and, for the moment, satisfied it. "You're sure about that?"

"Yes, I'm positive, so I suggest you place all your concentration on winning your son over and forget about your son's mother."

As he turned to cross the room to leave, he knew that he would never be able to forget about his son's mother, not in a million years. Before walking out the door he looked back at her. "Oh, yeah, I almost forgot something."

She lifted a brow. "What?"

"The brothers four. They're dying to see you. I told them of our plans for AJ and they agreed to be patient about seeing him, but they refuse to be patient about seeing you, Shelly. They want to know if you'll meet them for lunch one day this week at Chase's restaurant in downtown Atlanta?"

She smiled. She wanted to see them as well. Dare's brothers had always been special to her. "Tell them I'd love to have lunch with them tomorrow since I'll be working in that area."

Dare nodded, then turned and walked out the door.

AJ saw the two boys standing next to his bike the moment he walked out the school door. Since his bike was locked, he wasn't worried about the pair taking it, but after his fight with Caleb Martin yesterday the last thing he wanted was trouble. Especially after the talks the sheriff and his mother had given him.

The sheriff.

He shook his head, not wanting to think about the fact that the sheriff was his father. But he had thought about it most of the day, and still, as he'd told his mother last night, he didn't want the sheriff to know he was his son.

"What are you two looking at?" he asked in a tough voice, ignoring the fact that one of the boys was a lot bigger than he was.

"Your bike," the smaller of the two said, turning to him. "We think it's cool. Where did you get it?"

AJ relaxed. He thought his bike was cool, too. "Not from any place around here. My mom bought it for me in California."

"Is that where you're from?" the largest boy asked.

"Yeah, L.A. that's where I was born, and I hope we move back there." He sized up the two and decided they were harmless. He had seen them before around school, but neither had made an attempt to be friendly to him until now. "My name is AJ Brockman. What's yours?"

"My name is Morris Sears," the smaller of the two said, "and this is my friend Cornelius Thomas."

AJ nodded. "Do you live around here?"

"Yeah, just a few blocks, not far from Kate's Diner."

"I live just a few blocks from Kate's Diner, too, on Sycamore Street," AJ said, glad to know there were other kids living not far away.

"We saw what happened with you and Caleb Martin

yesterday," Morris said, his eyes widening. "Boy! Did you teach him a lesson! No one has ever done that before and we're glad, since he's been messing with people for a long time for no reason. He's nothing but a bully."

AJ nodded, agreeing with them.

"Would you like to ride home with us today?" Cornelius asked, getting on his own bike. We know a short cut that goes through the Millers' land. We saw a couple of deer on their property yesterday."

AJ's eyes lit up. He'd never seen a deer before, at least not a real live one. He then remembered where he had to go after school. "I'm sorry but today I can't. I have to report directly to the sheriff's office now."

"For fighting yesterday?" Morris asked.

AJ shook his head. "No, for cutting school two days ago. I was throwing rocks at cars and the sheriff caught me and took me in."

Cornelius eyes widened. "You got to ride in the back of Sheriff Westmoreland's car?" he asked excitedly.

AJ raised a brow. "Yes."

"Boy, that's cool. Sheriff Westmoreland is a hero."

AJ gave a snort of laughter. "A hero? And what makes him a hero? He's nothing but a sheriff who probably does nothing but sit in his office all day."

Morris and Cornelius shook their head simultaneously.

"Not Sheriff Westmoreland," Morris said as if he knew that for a fact. "He was in all the newspapers last week for catching those two bad guys the FBI has been looking for. My dad says Sheriff Westmoreland got shot at bringing them in and that a bullet barely missed his head."

"Yeah, and my dad said," Cornelius piped in, "that those bad guys didn't know who they were messing with, since everyone knows the sheriff doesn't play. Why, he used to even be an FBI agent. My dad went to school with him and graduated the same year Thorn Westmoreland did."

AJ looked curiously at Cornelius. "What does Thorn Westmoreland have to do with anything?"

Cornelius lifted a shocked brow. "Don't you know who Thorn Westmoreland is?"

Of course AJ knew who Thorn Westmoreland was. What kid didn't? "Sure. He's the motorcycle racer who builds the baddest bikes on earth."

Cornelius and Morris nodded. "He's also the sheriff's brother," Morris said grinning, happy to be sharing such news with their new friend. "And have you ever heard of Rock Mason?"

"The man who writes those adventure-thriller books?" AJ asked, his mind still reeling from what he'd just been told—Thorn Westmoreland was the sheriff's brother!

"Yes, but Rock Mason's real name is Stone Westmoreland and he's the sheriff's brother, too. Then there are two more of them, Chase and Storm Westmoreland. Mr. Chase owns a big restaurant downtown and Mr. Storm is a fireman."

AJ nodded. He wondered how Morris and Cornelius knew so much about a family that he was supposed to be a part of, yet he didn't know a thing about.

"And I forgot to mention that their sister married a prince from one of those faraway countries," Morris added, interrupting AJ's thoughts.

"How do you two know so much about the Westmorelands?" AJ asked, wrinkling his forehead.

"Because the sheriff coaches our Little League team and his brothers often help out."

"The sheriff coaches a baseball team?" AJ asked, thinking now he'd heard just about everything. The only time the people in L.A. saw the sheriff was when something bad happened and he was needed to make a statement on TV.

"Yes, and we're on the team and bring home the trophies every year. If you're good he might let you join."

AJ shrugged, not wanting to be around the sheriff any more than he had to. "No thanks, I don't want to join," he said. "Well, I've got to go, since I can't be late."

"How long do you have to go there?" Morris asked standing aside to let AJ get to his bike.

"The rest of the week, so I'll be free to ride home with you guys starting Monday if you still want me to," AJ said, getting on his bike.

"Yes," Cornelius answered. "We'll still want you, too. What about this weekend? Will your parents let you go look at the deer with us this weekend? Usually Mr. Miller gives his permission for us to come on his property as long as we don't get into any trouble."

AJ was doubtful. "I'll let you know tomorrow if I can go. My mom is kind of protective. She doesn't like me going too far from home."

Morris and Cornelius nodded in understanding. "Our moms are that way, too," Morris said. "But everyone around here knows the Millers. Your mom can ask the sheriff about them if she wants. They're nice people."

"Do you want to ride to school with us tomorrow?" Cornelius asked anxiously. "We meet at Kate's Diner every morning at seven-thirty, and she gives us a carton of chocolate milk free as long as we're good in school."

"Free chocolate milk? Hey, I'd like that. I'll see you guys in the morning." AJ put his bike into gear and headed for the sheriff's office, determined not to be late for a second time.

Six

Her mouth still knew him.

A multitude of emotions tightened Dare's chest as he sat at his desk and thought about the kiss he and Shelly had shared. Very slowly and very deliberately, he took his finger and rubbed it across his lips, lips that less than an hour ago had tasted sweetness of the most gut-wrenching kind. It was the kind of sweetness that made you crave something so delightful and pleasurable that it could become habit forming.

But what got to him more than anything was the fact that even after ten years, her mouth still knew him. That much was evident in the way her lips had molded to his, the familiarity of the way she had parted her mouth and the ease in which his tongue had slid inside, staking a claim he hadn't known he had a right to make until he had felt her response.

He leaned back in the chair. When it came to respond-

ing to him, that was something Shelly could never hold
back from doing. He'd always gotten the greatest pleasure
and enjoyment from hearing the sound of her purring in
bed. He used to know just what areas on her body to touch,
to caress and to taste. Often, all it took was a look, him simply meeting her gaze with deep desire and longing in his
eyes, and she would release an indrawn sigh that let him
know she knew just what he wanted and what he considered necessary. Those had been the times he hadn't been
able to keep his hands off her, and now it seemed, ten years
later, he still couldn't. And it didn't help matters any that
she had kissed him as though there hadn't been another
man inside her mouth in the ten years they'd been apart.
Her mouth had ached for his, demanded everything his
tongue could deliver, and he'd given it all, holding nothing back. He could have kept on kissing her for days.

Dare ran his hand over his face trying to see if doing so
would help him retain his senses. Kissing Shelly had affected him greatly. His body had been aching and throbbing since then, and the painful thing was that he didn't see
any relief in sight.

Over the past ten years he had dated a number of
women. His sister Delaney had even painted him and his
brothers as womanizers. But he felt that was as far from
the truth as it could be. After he and Shelly had broken up,
he'd been very selective about what women he wanted in
his bed. For years he had looked for Shelly's replacement,
only to discover such a woman didn't exist. He hadn't met
a woman who would hold a light to her, and he'd accepted
that and moved on. The women he'd slept with had been
there for the thrill, the adventure, but all he'd gotten was
the agony of defeat upon realizing that none could make
him feel in bed the way he'd always felt with Shelly. Oh,
he had experienced pleasure, but not the kind that made

you pound your chest with your fists and holler out for more. Not the kind that compelled you to go ahead and remain inside her body since another orgasm was there on the horizon. And not the kind you could still shudder from days later, just thinking about it.

He could only get those feelings with Shelly.

Closing his eyes, Dare remembered how she had broken off their kiss and the words she'd said before he'd left her house. *"You're AJ's father, but what was between us is over and has been for years. To me you're just another man."*

He sighed deeply and reopened his eyes. If Shelly believed that then she was wrong. Granted, AJ was their main concern, but what she didn't know and what he wouldn't tell her just yet was that his mission also included her. He hadn't realized until she had walked into his office two days ago that his life had been without direction for ten years. Seeing her, finding out about AJ and knowing that he and Shelly were still attracted to each other made him want something he thought he would never have again.

Peace and happiness.

The buzzer interrupted his thoughts. Leaning forwarding he pushed the button for the speaker-phone. "Yeah, Holly, what is it?"

"That Brockman kid is here, Sheriff. Do you want me to send him in?"

Dare again sighed deeply. "Yes, send him in."

Dare felt AJ watching him. The kid had been doing so off and on since he'd finished the chores he'd been assigned and had come into his office to sit at a table in the corner and finish his homework.

Dare had sat behind his desk, reading over various reports. The only sound in the room was AJ turning the pages of his science book and Dare shuffling the pages of the report. More than once Dare had glanced up and caught the kid looking at him, as if he were a puzzle he was trying to figure out. As soon as he'd been caught staring, the kid had quickly lowered his eyes.

Dare wondered what was going through AJ's mind now that he knew he was his father? The only reason Dare could come up with as to why he'd been studying him so intently was that he was trying to find similarities in their features. They were there. Even Holly had noticed them, although she hadn't said anything, merely moving her gaze between Dare and AJ several times before comprehension appeared on her face.

Dare glanced up and caught AJ staring again and decided to address the issue. "Is something wrong?" he asked.

AJ glanced up from his science book and glared at him. "What makes you think something is wrong?"

Dare shrugged. "Because I've caught you staring several times today like I've suddenly grown two heads or something."

He saw the corners of AJ lips being forced not to smile. "I hate being here. Why couldn't I just go home after I finished everything I had to do instead of hanging around here?"

"Because your punishment was to come here for an hour after school and I intend to get my hour. Besides, if I let you leave earlier, you might think I'm turning soft."

"That will be the day," AJ mumbled.

Dare chuckled and went back to reading his reports.

"Is Thorn Westmoreland really your brother?"

Dare lifted his head and gazed back across the room at AJ. My brother and your uncle, he wanted to say. Instead he responded by asking. "Who told you that?"

AJ shrugged. "Morris and Cornelius."

Dare nodded. He knew Morris and Cornelius. The two youngsters usually hung together and were the same age and went to the same school as AJ. "So you know Morris and Cornelius?"

AJ turned the page on his book before answering, pretending the response was being forced from him. "Yeah, I know them. We met today after school."

Dare nodded again. Morris and Cornelius were good kids. He knew their parents well and was glad the pair were developing a friendship with AJ, since he considered them a good influence. Both got good grades in school, sung in the youth choir at church and were active in a number of sports he and his brothers coached.

"Well, is he?"

Dare heard the anxiousness in AJ's voice, although the kid was trying to downplay it. "Yes, Thorn's my brother."

"And Rock Mason is, too?"

"Yes. I told you the other day I had four brothers and all of them live in this area."

AJ nodded. "And they help you coach your baseball team?"

Dare leaned back in his chair. "Yes, pretty much, although Thorn contributes to the youth of the community by teaching a special class at the high school on motorcycle safety and Stone is involved with the Teach People to Read program for both the young and old."

AJ nodded again. "What about the other two?"

Dare wondered at what point AJ would discover they were holding a conversation and revert back to his, I-don't-like-cops syndrome? Well, until he did, Dare planned to milk the situation for all it was worth. "Chase owns a restaurant and coaches a youth basketball team during basketball season. His team won the state championship two years in a row."

Dare smiled when he thought of his younger brother Storm. "My youngest brother Storm hasn't found his niche yet." Other than with women, Dare decided not to add. "So he helps me coach my baseball team and he also helps Chase with his basketball team."

"And your sister married a prince?"

Dare's smile widened when he thought of the baby sister he and his brothers simply adored. "Yes, although at the time we weren't ready to give her up."

AJ's eyes grew wider. "Why? Girls don't marry princes every day?"

Dare chuckled. "Yes, that may be true, but the Westmorelands have this unspoken code when it comes to family. We stick together and claim what's ours. Since Delaney was the only girl, we claimed her when she was born and weren't ready to give her up to anyone, including a prince."

AJ turned a few pages again, pretending further disinterest. A few moments later he asked. "What about your parents?"

Dare met AJ's stare. "What about them?"

"Do they live around here?"

"Yes, they live within walking distance. Their only complaint is that none of us, other than Delaney, have gotten married. They're anxious for grandkids and since they don't see Delaney's baby that often, they would like one of us to settle down and have a family."

Dare knew that what he'd just shared with AJ would get the kid to thinking. He was about to say something else when the buzzer on his desk sounded.

"Yes, McKade, what is it?"

"Ms. Brockman is here to see you."

Dare was surprised. He hadn't expected Shelly to drop by, since AJ had ridden his bike over from school. A quick glance across the room and he could tell by AJ's features that he was surprised by his mother's unexpected visit as well. "Send her in, McKade."

Dare stood as Shelly breezed into his office, dressed in a skirt and a printed blouse. "I hate to drop in like this, but I received an emergency call from one of my patients living in Stone Mountain and need to go out on a call. Ms. Kate has agreed to take care of AJ, and I have to drop him off at her place on my way out. I thought coming to pick him up would be okay since his hour is over."

Dare glanced at the clock on the wall which indicated AJ's hour had been over ten minutes ago. At some point the kid had stopped watching the clock and so had he.

"Since you're in a rush, I can save you the time by dropping him off at Ms. Kate's myself. I was getting ready to leave anyway."

Dare then remembered that since tonight was Wednesday night, his parents' usual routine was to have dinner with their five sons at Chase's restaurant before going to prayer meeting at church. He knew his family would love meeting AJ, and since they'd been told of his and Shelly's strategy about AJ knowing Dare was his father, there was no risk of someone giving anything away.

"And I have another idea," he said, meeting Shelly's gaze, trying not to notice how beautiful her eyes were, how beautiful she was, period. Just being in the same room with her had his mouth watering. She stood in the middle of his office silhouetted by the light coming in through his window and he thought he hadn't seen anything that looked this good in a long time.

"What?" she asked, interrupting his thoughts.

"AJ is probably hungry and I was on my way to Chase's restaurant where my family is dining tonight. He's welcome to join us, and I can drop him off at Ms. Kate's later."

Shelly nodded. Evidently Dare felt he'd made some headway with AJ for him to suggest such a thing. She glanced across the room at AJ who had his eyes glued to his book, pretending not have heard Dare's comment, although she knew that he had.

"AJ, Dare has invited you to dine with his family before dropping you off at Ms. Kate's. All right?"

It seemed AJ stared at her for an endless moment, as if weighing her words. He then shifted his gaze to Dare, and Shelly felt the sudden clash of two very strong personalities, two strong-willed individuals, two people who were outright stubborn. But then she saw something else, something that met her breath catch and her heart do a flip—two individuals who, for whatever reason, were silently agreeing to a give a little, at least for this one particular time.

AJ then shifted his gaze back to her. He shrugged. "Whatever."

Shelly let out a deep sigh. "Okay, then, I'll see you later." She walked across the room to place a kiss on AJ's forehead; ignoring the frown he gave her. "Behave yourself tonight," she admonished.

She turned and smiled at Dare before walking out of his office.

"The only reason I decided to come with you is because I want to meet Thorn Westmoreland. I think he is so cool." AJ said, and then turned his attention back to the scenery outside the vehicle's window.

Instead of using the police cruiser, Dare had decided to drive his truck instead, the Chevy Avalanche he'd purchased a month ago. He glanced over at AJ when he brought the vehicle to a stop at a traffic light. He couldn't help but chuckle. "I figured as much, but you won't be the first kid who tried getting on my good side just to meet Thorn."

AJ scowled. "I'm not trying to get on your good side," he mumbled."

Dare chuckled again. "Oh, sorry. My mistake."

For the next couple of miles the inside of the vehicle was quiet as Dare navigated through evening traffic with complete ease.

"So, how was your day at school?" Dare decided to ask when the vehicle finally came to a complete standstill as he attempted to get on the interstate.

AJ glanced over at him. "It had its moments."

Dare smiled. "What kind of moments?"

AJ glared. "Why are you asking me all these questions?"

Dare met his gaze. "Because I'm interested."

AJ's glare deepened. "Are you interested in me or in my mother? I saw the way you were looking at her."

Dare decided the kid was too observant, although he was falling in nicely with their plans. "And what way was I looking at her?"

"One of those man-like-woman looks."

Dare chuckled, never having heard it phased quite that way before. "What do you know about a man-like-woman look?"

"I wasn't born yesterday."

"Not for one minute did I think you had been." After a few moments he glanced back at AJ. "Did you know your mom used to be my girlfriend some years back?"

"So?"

"So, I thought you should know."

"Why?"

"Because she was very special to me then."

When Dare exited off the interstate, AJ spoke. "That was back then. My mother doesn't need a boyfriend, if that's what you're thinking."

Dare gave his son a smile when he brought the vehicle to a stop at a traffic light. "What I think, AJ, is that you should let your mom make her own decisions about those kinds of things."

AJ glared at him. "I don't like you."

Dare shrugged and gave his son a smile. "Then I guess that means nothing has changed." But he knew something *had* changed. As far as he was concerned, AJ consenting to go to dinner with him to meet his family was a major breakthrough. And although the kid claimed that Thorn was the only reason he was going, Dare had no problem using his brother to his advantage if that's what it took. Besides, AJ would soon discover that of all the Westmorelands, Thorn was the one who was biggest on family ties and devotion, and if you accepted one Westmoreland, you basically accepted them all, since they were just that thick.

At that moment Dare's cell phone rang and he answered it. After a few remarks and nods of his head, he said. "You're welcome to join us for dinner if you'd like. I know for a fact that everyone would love to see you." He nodded again and said, "All right. I'll see you later.

Moments later he glanced over at AJ when they came to a stop in front of Chase's restaurant. "That was your mother. The emergency wasn't as bad as she'd thought, and she is on her way back home. I'm to take you there after dinner instead of to Ms. Kate's house.

AJ narrowed his eyes at Dare. "Why did you do that?"

"Do what?" Dare asked, lifting a brow.

"Invite her to dinner?"

"Because I figured that like you, she has to eat sometime, and I know that my family would have love seeing her again." He hesitated for a few moments, then added. "And I would have liked seeing her again myself. Like I said, your mom used to mean a lot to me a long time ago."

Their gazes locked for a brief moment, then AJ glared at him and said angrily. "Get over it."

Dare smiled slightly. "I don't know if I can." Before AJ

had time to make a comeback, Dare unsnapped his seatbelt. "Come on, it's time to go inside."

Shelly pulled onto the interstate, hoping and praying that AJ was on his best behavior. No matter what, she had to believe that all the lessons in obedience, honor and respect that he'd been taught at an early age were somewhere buried beneath all that hostility he exhibited at times. But right now she had to cope with the fact that he was still a child, a child who was getting older each day and enduring growing pains of the worst kind. But one thing was for certain, Dare was capable of dealing with it, and for that she was grateful.

When she thought of Dare, she had no choice but to think of her traitorous body and the way it had responded to him earlier that day at her house. As she'd told AJ, Dare was smart. He was also very receptive, and she knew he had picked up on the fact that she had wanted him. All it had taken was one mind-blowing kiss and she'd been ready to get naked if he'd asked.

When she came to a traffic light she momentarily closed her eyes, asking for strength where Dare was concerned. If she allowed him to become a part of her life, she could be asking for potential heartbreak all over again, although she had to admit the new Dare seemed more settled, less likely to go chasing after some other dream. But whatever the two of them had once shared was in the past, and she refused to bring it to the present. She had enough to deal with in handling AJ without trying to take on his father, too.

She had to continue to make it clear to Dare that it was his son he needed to work on and win over and not her. Their first and foremost concern was AJ, and no matter how hot and bothered she got around Dare, she would not give in again. She had to watch her steps and not put any ideas into Dare's head. More than anything, she had to stop looking at him and thinking about sex.

Her body was doing a good job reminding her that ten years was a long time to go without. She'd been too busy for the abstinence to cross her mind, but today Dare had awakened desires she'd thought were long buried. Now she felt that her body was under attack—against her. It was demanding things she had no intention of delivering.

Her breath caught and she felt her nipples tingle as she again thought about the kiss they had shared. Once more she prayed for the strength and fortitude to deal with Alisdare Julian Westmoreland.

Seven

"Dad, Mom, I'd like you to meet, AJ. He's Shelly's boy." Dare knew his father wouldn't give anything away, but he wasn't so convinced about his mother as he saw the play of emotions that crossed her features. She was looking into the face of a grandson she hadn't known she'd had; a grandson she was very eager to claim.

Luckily for Dare, his father understood the strategy that he and Shelly were using with AJ and spoke up before his wife had a chance to react to the emotions she was trying to hold inside. "You're a fine-looking young man, but I would expect no less coming from Shelly." He reached out and touched AJ's shoulder and smiled. "I'm glad you're joining us for dinner. How's your mother?"

"She's fine," AJ said quietly, bowing his head and studying his shoes.

Dare wondered what kind of docile act the kid was performing, but then another part of him wondered if when taken out of his comfort zone, AJ had a tendency to feel uneasy around people he didn't know. Dare recalled a conversation he'd had with Shelly about AJ not being all that outgoing.

When Dare saw Thorn enter the restaurant he beckoned him over saying, "Thorn, I'd like you to meet someone. From what I gather, he's a big fan of yours."

AJ's mouth literally fell open and the size of his eyes increased. He tilted his head back to gaze up at the man towering over him. "Wow! You're Thorn Westmoreland!"

Thorn gave a slow grin. "Yes, I'm Thorn Westmoreland. Now who might you be?"

To Dare's surprise, AJ grinned right back. It was the first look of happiness he'd seen on his son's face, and a part of him regretted he hadn't been the one to put it there.

"I'm AJ Brockman."

Thorn tapped his chin with his finger a couple of times as if thinking about something. "Brockman. Brockman. I used to know a Shelly Brockman some years ago. In fact she used to be Dare's girlfriend. Are you related to that Brockman?"

"Yes, I'm her son."

Thorn chuckled. "Well, I'll be," he said, pretending he didn't already know that fact. "And how's your mother?"

"She's fine."

At that moment Dare looked up and saw his other brothers enter. More introductions were made, and, just like Thorn, they pretended they were surprised to see AJ, and no one gave anything away about knowing he was Dare's son.

When they all sat down to eat, with AJ sitting between Thorn and Dare, it was obvious to anyone who cared to notice that the boy was definitely a Westmoreland.

Shelly put aside the novel she'd been reading when she heard the doorbell ring. A glance out the peephole confirmed it was AJ, but he wasn't alone. Dare had walked him to the door, and with good reason. AJ was half asleep and barely standing on his feet.

She quickly opened the door to AJ's mumblings. "I told you I could walk to the door myself without your help," he was saying none too happily.

"Yeah, and I would have watched you fall on your face, too," was Dare's response

Shelly stepped aside and let them both enter. "How was dinner?" she asked, closing the door behind them.

AJ didn't answer, instead he continued walking and headed for the stairs. She gave a quick glance to Dare, who was watching AJ as he tried maneuvering the stairs. "That kid is so sleepy he can't think straight," he said. "You might want to help him before he falls and breaks his neck. I would do it, but I think he's had enough of me for one evening."

Shelly nodded, then quickly provided AJ a shoulder to lean on while he climbed the stairs.

Dare moved to stand at the foot of the stairs and watched Shelly and AJ until they were no longer in sight. He sighed deeply, thinking how his adrenaline had pumped up when Shelly had opened the door. She'd been wearing the same outfit she'd worn to his office that evening, and his gaze had been glued to her backside all the while she'd moved up the stairs, totally appreciating the sway of her hips and the way the skirt intermittently slid up her thighs with each upward step she took.

He thought that he would do just about anything to be able to follow right behind her and tumble her straight into bed, but he knew that wasn't possible, especially with AJ in the house. Not to mention the fact that she was still acting rather cautiously around him.

He knew it would probably take her a while to get AJ ready for bed, and since he didn't intend leaving until they had talked, he decided to sit on the sofa and wait for her. He picked up the book she'd been reading, Stone's most recent bestseller, and smiled, thinking it was a coincidence that he was reading the same book.

Making sure he kept the spot where she'd stopped reading marked, he flipped a couple of chapters ahead and picked up where he'd left off last night before sleep had overtaken him.

Shelly paused on the middle stair when she noticed Dare sitting on her sofa reading the book she had begun reading earlier that day. She couldn't help noticing that her living room appeared quiet and seductive, and the light from a floor lamp next to where he sat illuminated his features and created an alluring scene that was too enticing to ignore.

She silently studied him for a long time, wondering just how many peaceful moments he was used to getting as sheriff. He looked comfortable, relaxed and just plain sexy as sin. His features were calm, yet she could tell by the way his eyes were glued to the page that he was deeply absorbed in the action-thriller novel his brother had written.

He shifted in his seat while turning the page and crossed one leg over the other. She knew they were strong legs, sturdy legs, legs that had held her body in place while his had pumped relentlessly into her, legs that had nudged hers apart again when he wanted a second round and a third.

Swallowing at the memory, she felt her heart rate increase, and decided the best way to handle Dare was to send him home—real quick-like. She didn't think she could handle another episode like the one they had shared earlier that day.

He must have heard the sound of her heavy breathing, or maybe she had let out a deep moan without realizing she'd uttered a single word. Something definitely gave her away, and she felt heat pool between her legs when he lifted his gaze from the book and looked at her. It wasn't just an ordinary look either. It was a hot look, a definite scorcher and a blatant, I-want-to-take-you-to-bed look.

She blinked, thinking she had misread the look, but then she knew she hadn't. He wouldn't say the words out loud, but he definitely wanted her to know what he was thinking. She breathed in deeply. Dare was trouble and she was determined to send him packing.

He stood when she took the last few steps down the stairs. "He's out like a light," she said quietly when he came to stand in front of her. "I could barely get him in the shower and in bed without him falling asleep again. Thanks for taking him to dinner and for making sure he got back home."

Shelly paused, knowing she had just said a mouthful, but she wasn't through yet. "I know you've had a busy day today and need your rest as much as I do, so I'll see you out now. In fact you didn't have to wait around for me to finish upstairs."

"Yes, I did."

She stared at him. "Why?"

"I thought you'd want to know how tonight went."

Shelly inwardly groaned. Of course she wanted to know how tonight went, but she'd been so intent on getting Dare out the door she had forgotten to ask. "Yes, of course. Did he behave himself? How did he take to your family?"

Dare glanced up at the top of the stairs then returned his gaze to her. "Is there somewhere we can talk privately?"

The first place Shelly thought about was the kitchen, and then she remembered what had happened between them earlier that day. She decided the best place to talk would be outside on the porch. That way he would definitely be out of the house. "We can talk outside on the porch," she said, moving in that direction.

Without waiting for his response, she took the few steps to the door and stepped outside.

The night air was crisp and clear. The first thing Shelly noticed was the full moon in the sky, and the next was the zillions of stars that sparkled like diamonds surrounding it. She went to stand next to a porch post, since it was the best spot for the glow of light from the moon. The last thing she needed was to stand in some dark area of the porch with Dare.

She heard him behind her when he joined her, however, instead of standing with her in the light, he went and sat in the porch swing that was located in a darkened corner. She sucked in a breath. If he thought for one minute that she would join him in that swing, he had another thought coming. As far as she was concerned, they could converse just fine right where they were.

"So how did AJ behave tonight?" she asked, deciding to plunge right in, since there was no reason to prolong the moment.

She heard the swing's slow rocking when he replied. "To my surprise, very well. In fact, his manners were impeccable, but then it was obvious that he was trying to impress Thorn." Dare chuckled "He pretty much tried ignoring me, but my brothers picked up on what he was doing and wrecked those plans. Whenever he tried excluding me from the conversation, they counteracted and included me. Pretty soon he gave up, after finding out the hard way an important lesson about the Westmorelands."

"Which is?"

"We stick together, no matter what."

Shelly nodded. She'd known that from previous years. "But I must admit there was this one time when they were ready to disclaim me as their brother," Dare said, chuckling.

Shelly rested her back against the post and crossed her legs. "And what time was that?"

"The night I ended things with you. They thought I was crazy to give you up for any reason. And that included a career."

She nervously rubbed her hands up and down her arms, not wanting to talk about what used to be between them. "Well, all that's in the past, Dare. Is there anything else about tonight I should know?" she asked, trying to keep their conversation moving along.

"Yes, there is something else."

She sought out his features, but could barely make them out in the darkened corner of the porch. "What?"

"I gave AJ reason to believe that I'm interested in you again."

Shelly nodded. "And how did he handle that?"

Dare smiled. "He had something to say about it, if that's what you're asking. Just how far he'll go to make sure nothing develops between us I can't rightly say."

Shelly nodded again. Neither could she. Personally, she thought AJ's dislike of Dare was a phase he was going through, but a very important phase in his life, and she didn't want to do anything to make things worse with him. "In that case, more than likely he'll have a talk with me about it."

Dare leaned back against the swing. "And what do you plan to say when he does?"

Shelly sighed. "Basically, everything we agreed I should say. I'm to let him know he's the one who has a beef with you, not me, and therefore I don't have a problem with re-establishing our relationship."

Dare heard her words. Although they were fabricated for

AJ's benefit, they sounded pretty damn good to him, and he wished they were true, because he certainly didn't have a problem reestablishing anything with her.

He looked over at Shelly and saw how she leaned against the post while silhouetted by the glow from the moon. His gaze zeroed on the fact that she stood with her legs crossed. Tight. She had once told him that she had a tendency to stand with her legs crossed really tight whenever she felt a deep throbbing ache between them. Evidently she had forgotten sharing that piece of information with him some years ago.

"Well, if that about covers everything, then we'd best call it a night."

Her words interrupted his thought, and he figured they could do better than just call it a night. Calling it a "night of seduction" sounded more to his liking. Some inner part of him wanted to know if she wanted him as much as he wanted her, and there was only one way to find out.

"Come sit with me for a while, Shelly," he said, his voice husky.

Shelly swallowed and met his gaze. "I don't think that's a good idea, Dare."

"I do. It's a beautiful night and I think we should enjoy it before saying goodnight."

Enjoy it or enjoy each other? Shelly was tempted to ask, but decided she wouldn't go there with Dare. Once he got her in that swing that would be the end of it. Or the beginning of it, depending on the way you looked at it. Her body was responding to him in the most unsettled and provocative way tonight. All he had to do was to touch her one time and…

"Let me give you what you need, Shelly."

He saw her chin lift defiantly, and he saw the way she frowned at him. "And what makes you think that you know what I need?"

"Your legs."

She raised a confused brow. "What about my legs?"

"They're crossed, and pretty damn tight."

Shelly's heart missed a beat and the throbbing between her legs increased. He had remembered. A long, seemingly endless moment of silence stretched out between them. She could see his features. They were as tight as her legs were crossed. And the gaze that held hers was like a magnet, drawing her in, second by tantalizing second.

She shook her head, trying to deny her body what it wanted, what it evidently needed, but it had a mind of its own and wasn't adhering to any protest she was making. The man sitting on the swing watching her, waiting for her, had a history of being able to pleasure her in every possible way. He knew it and she knew it as well.

Breathing deeply, she found herself slowly crossing the porch toward him, out of the light and into the darkness, out from temptation and into a straight path that led to seduction. She came to a stop between his spread knees and when their legs touched, she sucked in a deep breath at the same time she heard him suck in one, too. And when she felt his hand reach under her skirt skimming her inner thigh, her knees almost turned to mush.

His voice was husky and ultra sexy when he spoke. "This morning I had to know if your mouth still knew me. Now I want to find out if this," he said, gliding his warm hand upward, boldly touching the crotch of her panties, "knows me as well."

Her eyes fluttered closed and she automatically reached out and placed both hands on his shoulders for support. A part of her wanted to scream Yes! Her body knew him as the last man...the only man...to stake a claim in this territory, but she was incapable of speech. All she could do was stand there and wait to see what would happen next and hope she could handle it.

She didn't have to wait long; the tips of Dare's fingers slowly began messaging the essence of her as he relentlessly stroked his hand over the center of her panties.

"You're hot, Shelly," he said, his voice huskier than before. "Sit down in my lap facing me."

Dare had to move his body forward then sideways for her to accommodate his request. The arrangement brought her face just inches from his. His hand was still between her legs.

He leaned forward and captured her mouth, giving her a kiss that made the one they'd shared that morning seemed complacent. Her senses became frenzied and aroused, and the feel of his hand stroking her only added to her turmoil. And when she felt his fingers inch past the edge of her bikini panties, she released a deep moan.

"Yeah, baby, that's the sound I want to hear," he said after releasing her lips. "Open your legs a little wider and tell me how you like this."

Before she could completely comply with his request, he slid three fingers inside her, and when he found that too tight a fit, backed out and went with two. "You're pretty snug in there, baby," he whispered as his fingers began moving in and out of her in a rhythm meant to drive her insane. "How do you like this?"

"I love it," she whispered, clenching his shoulders with her hands. "Oh, Dare, it's been so long."

He leaned closer and traced the tips of her lips with his tongue before moving to nibble at her ear. She was about to go up in smoke, and he couldn't help but wonder how long it had been for her, since this was making her come apart so quickly and easily. He asked, "how long has it been, Shelly?"

She met his gaze and drew in a trembling breath. "Not since you, Dare."

His fingers went still; his jaw tightened and his gaze locked with hers. "You mean that you haven't done this since we..."

She didn't let him finished as she closed her mouth over his, snatching his words and his next breath in the process. But the thought that no other man had touched her since him sent his mind escalating, his entire body trembling. No wonder her legs had been crossed so tightly and he intended to make it good for her.

His fingers began moving inside her again and her muscles automatically clenched around them. She was tight and wet and the scent of her arousal was driving him insane. He broke off the kiss, desperately needing to taste her.

"Unbutton your top, Shelly."

She released her hands from his shoulders and slowly unbuttoned her blouse, then unsnapped the front opening of her bra. As soon as her breasts poured forth, looming before him, he began sucking, nibbling and licking his way to heaven. He moved his fingers within her using the same rhythm his tongue was using on her breasts.

He felt the moment her body shook and placed his mouth over hers to absorb her moans of pleasure when spasms tore into her. Her fingernails dug into his shoulders as he continued using his fingers to pleasure her. And when it started all over again, and more spasms rammed through her, signaling a second orgasm, she pulled her mouth from his, closed her eyes and leaned forward to his chest, crying out into the cotton of his shirt.

"That's it baby, let go and enjoy."

And as another turbulent wave of pleasure ripped through her and she fought to catch her breath, Shelly let go and enjoyed every single moment of what Dare was doing to her.

And she doubted that after tonight her life would ever be the same.

Eight

"Mom? Mom? Are you okay?"

Shelly heard the sound of AJ's voice as he tried gently to shake her awake.

"Mom, wake up. Please say something."

She quickly opened her eyes when her mind registered the panic in his tone. She blinked, feeling dazed and disoriented, and tried to focus on him, but at the moment she felt completely wrung out. "AJ? What are you doing out of bed?"

Confusion appeared in his face. "Mom, I'm supposed to be out of bed. It's morning and I have to go to school today. You forgot to wake me up. And why did you sleep on the sofa all night in the same clothes you had on yesterday?"

Somehow, Shelly found the strength to sit up. She yawned, feeling bone-tired. "It's morning already?" The last thing she remembered was having her fourth orgasm in Dare's arms and slumping against him without any strength left even to hold up her head. He must have brought her into the house and placed her on the sofa, thinking she would eventually come around and go up the stairs. Instead, exhausted, depleted and totally satisfied, she had slept through the night.

"Mom, are you all right?

She met AJ's concerned gaze. He had no idea just how all right she was. Dare had given her just what her body had needed. She had forgotten just what an ace he was with his fingers on a certain part of her. "Yes, AJ, I'm fine." She glanced at the coffee table and noticed the book both she and Dare had been reading and considered it the perfect alibi. "I must have fallen asleep reading. What time is it? You aren't late are you?" She leaned back against the sofa's cushions. After a night like last light, she could curl up and sleep for the entire day.

"No, I'm not late, but you might be if you have to go to work today."

Shelly shook her head. "I only have a couple of patients I need to see, and I hadn't planned on going anywhere until around ten." She decided not to mention that she was also having lunch with Dare's brothers today. She yawned again. "What would you like for breakfast?"

He shrugged. "I'll just have a bowl of cereal. I met these two guys at school yesterday and we're meeting up to ride our bikes together."

Shelly nodded. She hoped AJ hadn't associated himself with the wrong group again. "Who are these boys?"

"Morris Sears and Cornelius Thomas. And we're going to meet at Kate's Diner every morning for chocolate milk." As an afterthought he added. "And it's free if we let her know we've been good in school."

Shelly made a mental note to ask Dare about Morris and Cornelius when she saw him again. Being Sheriff he probably knew if the two were troublemakers.

"They're real cool guys and they like my bike," AJ went on to say. "Yesterday they told me all about the sheriff and his brothers." His eyes grew wide. "Why didn't you tell me that Thorn Westmoreland is my uncle?"

"Because he's not."

At AJ's confused frown, Shelly decided to explain. "Until you accept Dare as your father you can't claim any of the Westmorelands as your uncles."

AJ glared. "That doesn't seem fair."

"And why doesn't it? You're the one who doesn't want Dare knowing he's your father, so how can you tell anyone that Thorn and the others are your uncles without explaining the connection? Until you decide differently, to the Westmorelands you're just another kid."

She stood. "Now, I'm going upstairs and shower while you eat breakfast."

AJ nodded as he slowly walked out of the room and headed for the kitchen. Shelly knew she had given him something to think about.

"Is it true?" Morris asked excitedly the moment AJ got off his bike at Ms. Kate's Diner.

AJ raised a brow. "Is what true?"

It was Cornelius who answered, his wide, blue eyes expressive. "That you had dinner with the sheriff and his family last night?"

AJ shrugged, wondering how they knew that. "Yeah, so what about it?"

"We think it's cool, that's what about it. The sheriff is the bomb. He makes sure everyone in this town is safe at night. My mom and dad say so," Cornelius responded without wasting any time.

AJ and the two boys opened the door and walked into the diner. "How did you know I had dinner with the sher-

iff?" he asked as they walked up to the counter where car-
tons of chocolate milk had been placed for them.

"Mr. and Mrs. Turner saw all of you and called my
grandmother who then called my mom and dad. Everyone
was wondering who you were and I told my mom that you
were a kid who got in trouble and had to report to the sheriff's office after school every day. They thought you were
a family member or something, but I told them you
weren't."

AJ nodded. "My mom had to go to work unexpectedly
last night and the sheriff offered to take me to dinner with
him since I hadn't eaten."

"Wow! That was real nice of him, wasn't it?"

AJ hadn't really thought about it being an act of kindness and said, "Yeah, I guess so."

"Do you think he'll mind if we go with you to his office after school?" Morris asked excitedly.

AJ scrunched his face, thinking. "I guess not, but he
might put you to work."

Morris shrugged. "That's all right if he does. I just want
him to tell us about the time he was an FBI agent and did
that undercover stuff to catch the bad guys."

AJ nodded. He didn't want to admit it, but he wouldn't
mind hearing about that himself. He smiled when the nice
lady behind the counter handed them each a donut to go
along with their milk.

Shelly's hands tightened on the steering wheel after she
brought her car to a stop next to the police cruiser marked
Sheriff. She'd had no idea Dare would be joining his brothers for lunch. How would she manage a straight face
around him and not let anyone know they had spent close
to an hour in a darkened area of her porch last night doing
something deliriously naughty?

She opened the car door and took a deep breath, thinking that the things Dare had done to her had turned her inside out and whetted her appetite. To put it more bluntly, sixteen hours later she was still aroused. After having gone without sex for so long she now felt downright hungry. In fact *starving* was a better word to use. Would Dare look at her and detect her sexually-excited state? If anyone could, it would be Dare, a man who'd once known her better than she'd known herself.

And to think she'd even admitted to him that she hadn't slept with another soul since their breakup ten years ago. Now that he knew, she had to keep her head on straight and keep Dare's focus on AJ and not her.

With a deep sigh she opened the door and went inside.

She paused and watched all five men stand the moment she entered the restaurant. They must have seen her drive up and were ready to greet her. Tears burned the back of her eyes. It had been too long. When she'd been Dare's girlfriend, the brothers had claimed her as an honorary sister, and since she'd been an only child, she'd held that attachment very dear. One of the hardest things about leaving College Park had been knowing that in addition to leaving Dare she'd also left behind a family she had grown very close to.

As she looked at them now, she began to smile. They stood in a line as if awaiting royalty and she walked up to them, one by one. "Thorn," she said to the one closest to Dare in age. She gladly accepted the kiss he boldly placed on her lips and the hug he fondly gave her.

"Ten years is a long time to be gone, Shelly," he said with a serious expression on his face. "Don't try it again."

She couldn't help but smile upon seeing that he was bossy as ever. "I won't, Thorn."

She then moved to Stone, the first Westmoreland she

had come to know; the one who had introduced her to
Dare. Without saying a word she reached for him, hugging
him tightly. After they released each other, he placed a
kiss on her lips as well.

"I'm so proud of your accomplishments, Stone," she
said smiling through her tears. "And I buy every book you
write."

He chuckled. "Thanks, Shell." His face then grew serious. "And I ditto what Thorn said. Don't leave again." His
gaze momentarily left hers and shifted to where Dare was
standing. He glared at his brother before returning his gaze
to hers and added, "No matter what the reason."

She nodded. "All right."

Then came the twins, who were a year younger than she.
She remembered them getting into all sorts of mischief, and
from the gleams in their eyes, it was evident they were still
up to no good. After they both placed chaste pecks on her
lips, Storm said, smiling. "We told Dare that he blew his
chance with you, which means you're now available for us."

Shelly grinned. "Oh, am I?"

"Yeah, if you want to be," Chase said, teasingly, giving
her another hug.

When Chase released her she drew a deep breath. Next
came Dare.

"Dare," she acknowledged softly, nervously.

She figured since she'd already been in his company a few
times, not to mention what they had done together last night,
that he would not make a big production of seeing her. She
soon discovered just how wrong that assumption was when
he gently pulled her into his arms and captured her lips, nearly
taking her breath in the process. There was nothing chaste
about the kiss he gave her and she knew it had intentionally
lasted long enough to cause his brothers to speculate and to
give anyone who saw them kiss something to talk about.

When he released her mouth, it was Stone who decided to make light of what Dare had done by saying. "What was that about, Dare? Were you trying to prove to Shelly that you could still kiss?"

Dare answered as his gaze held hers. He smiled at Stone's comment and said. "Yeah, something like that."

Shelly never had problems getting through a meal before. But then she'd never had the likes of Dare Westmoreland on a mission to seduce her. And it didn't matter that she was sitting at a table in a restaurant next to him, surrounded by his brothers, or that the place was filled to lunch-crowd capacity.

She took several deep breaths to calm her racing heart, but it did nothing to soothe the ache throbbing through her. It all started when she caught herself staring at his hand as he lifted a water goblet to his lips. Seeing his fingers had reminded her how she had whimpered her way into ecstasy as those same fingers had stroked away ten years of sexual frustration.

She had caught his eyes dark with desire, over the water glass, and had realized he had read her thoughts. And, as smooth as silk, when he placed the glass down he took that same hand and without calling attention to what he was doing, placed it under the table on her thigh.

At first she'd almost jerked at the cool feel of his hand, then she'd relaxed when his hand just rested on her thigh without moving. But then, moments later, she had almost gasped when his hand moved to settle firmly between her legs. And amidst all conversations going on around them, as the brothers tried to bring her up to date on what had been going on in their lives over the past ten years, no one seemed to have noticed that one of Dare's hands was missing from the table while he gently stroked her slowly back and forth through the material of her shorts. He'd tried getting her zipper down, a zipper that, thanks to the way she was sitting, wouldn't budge.

Thinking that she had to do something, anything to stop this madness, she leaned forward and placed her elbows on the table and cupped her face in her hands as she tried to ignore the multitude of sensations flowing through her. She glanced around wondering if any of the brothers had any idea what Dare was up to, but from the way they were talking and eating, it seemed they had more on their minds than Dare not keeping his hands to himself.

"We want you to know that we'll do everything we can to help you with AJ, Shelly."

Shelly nodded at Stone's offer and then felt her cheeks grow warmer when another one of Dare's fingers wiggled its way inside her shorts. "I appreciate that, Stone."

"He's my responsibility," Dare spoke up and glanced at his brothers, keeping a straight face, not giving away just what sidebar activities he was engaged in.

"Yeah, but he belongs to us, too," Thorn said. "He's a Westmoreland, and I think that you did a wonderful job with him, Shelly, considering the fact that you've been a single parent for the past ten years. He's going through growing pains now, but once he sees that he has a family who cares deeply for him, he'll be just fine."

She nodded. She had to believe that as well. "Thanks, Thorn."

"Well, although I truly enjoyed all your company, it's time for me to get back to the station," Dare said, finally removing his hand from between her legs. When he stood she glanced up at him knowing that regardless of whether it was a dark, cozy corner on her porch at night or in a restaurant filled with people in broad day light, Dare Westmoreland did just what he pleased, and it seemed that nothing pleased him more than touching her.

"So, what did you do next, Sheriff?"

Dare shook his head. When AJ had shown up after school, he had brought Morris and Cornelius with him and explained that the two had wanted to tag along. Dare had made it clear that if they had come to keep AJ company then they might as well help him with the work, and he had just the project for the three of them.

He had taken them to the basement where the police youth athletic league's equipment was stored, with instructions that they bring order to the place. That past year a number of balls, gloves and bats had been donated by one of the local sports stores.

Deciding to stay and help as well to supervise, he had not been prepared for the multitude of questions that Morris and Cornelius were asking him. AJ didn't ask him anything, but Dare knew he was listening to everything that was being said.

"That's why it pays to be observant," Dare said, unloading another box. "It's always a clue when one guy goes inside and the other stays out in the car with the motor running. They had no idea I was with law enforcement. I pretended to finish filling my tank up with gas, and out of the corner of my eye I could see the man inside acting strangely and I knew without a doubt that a robbery was about to take place."

"Wow! Then what did you do?" Morris asked, with big, bright eyes.

"Although I worked for the Bureau, we had an unspoken agreement with the local authorities to make them aware of certain things and that's what I did. Pretending to be checking out a map, I used my cell phone to alert the local police of what was happening. The only reason I became involved was because I saw that one of the robbers intended to take a hostage, a woman who'd been inside paying for gas. At that point I knew I had to make a move."

"Weren't you afraid you might get hurt?" AJ asked.

Dare wondered if AJ was aware that he was now as engrossed in the story as Morris and Cornelius were. "No, AJ, at the time the only thing I could think about was that an innocent victim was at risk. Her safety became my main concern at that point, and whatever I did, I had to make sure that she wasn't hurt or injured."

"So what did you do?"

"In the pretense of paying for my gas, I entered the store at the same time the guy was forcing the woman out. I decided to use a few martial arts moves I had learned in the marines, and—"

"You used to be in the marines?" AJ asked.

Dare smiled. The look of total surprise and awe on his son's face was priceless. "Yes, I served in the marines for four years, right after college."

AJ smiled. "Wow!"

"My daddy says the marines only picks the most bravest and the best men," Morris said, also impressed.

Dare smiled. "I think all the branches of the military selects good men, but I do admit that marines are a very special breed." He glanced at his watch. "It's a little over an hour, guys. Do I need to call any of your parents to let them know that you're on your way home?"

All three boys shook their heads, indicating that Dare didn't have to. "All right."

"Sheriff, do you think you can teach us some simple martial arts moves?" Cornelius asked.

"Yeah, sheriff, with bad people kidnapping kids we need to know how to protect ourselves, don't we?" Morris chimed in.

Dare grinned when he saw AJ vigorously nodding his head, agreeing with Morris. "Yes, I guess that's something all of you should know, some real simple moves. Just as long as you don't use it on your classmates for fun or to try to show off."

"We wouldn't do that," Morris said eagerly.

Dare nodded. "All right then. I'll try to map out some time this Saturday morning. How about checking with your parents, and if they say it's all right, then the three of you can meet me here."

He glanced at his watch again. Shelly didn't know it yet, but he intended to see her again tonight, no matter what excuse he had to make to do so. He smiled, pleased with the progress he felt he'd made with AJ today. "Okay guys, let's get things moving so we can call it a day. The three of you did an outstanding job and I appreciate it."

"Mom, did you know that the sheriff used to be in the marines?"

Shelly glanced up from her book and met AJ's excited gaze. He was stretched out on the floor by the sofa doing his homework. "Yes, I knew that. We dated during that time."

"Wow!"

She lifted a brow. "What's so fantastic about him being a marine?"

AJ rolled his eyes to the ceiling. "Mom, everyone knows that marines are tough. They adapt, improvise and overcome!"

Shelly smiled at her son's Clint Eastwood imitation from one of his favorite movies. "Oh." She went back to reading her book.

"And Mom, he told us about the time he caught two men trying to rob a convenience store and taking a hostage with them. It was real cool how he captured the bad guys."

"Yeah, I'm sure it was."

"And he offered to teach us martial arts moves on Saturday morning at the police station so we'll know how to protect ourselves," he added excitedly in a forward rush.

Shelly lifted her head from her book again. "Who?"

"The sheriff."

She nodded. "Oh, your father?"

Their gazes locked and Shelly waited for AJ's comeback, expecting a denial that he did not consider Dare his father. After a few minutes he shrugged his shoulders and said softly, "Yes." He then quickly looked away and went back to doing his homework.

Shelly inhaled deeply. AJ admitting Dare was his father was a start. It seemed the ice surrounding his heart was slowly beginning to melt, and he was beginning to see Dare in a whole new light.

Nine

Dare walked into Coleman's Florist knowing that within ten minutes of the time he walked out, everyone in College Park would know he had sent flowers to Shelly. Luanne Coleman was one of the town's biggest gossips, but then he couldn't worry about that, especially since for once her penchant to gab would work in his favor. Before nightfall he wanted everyone to know that he was in hot pursuit of Shelly Brockman.

Due to the escape of a convict in another county, he had spent the last day and a half helping the sheriff of Stone Mountain track down the man. Now, thirty-six hours after the man had been recaptured, Dare was bone tired and regretted he had missed the opportunity to see Shelly two nights ago as he'd planned. The best he could do was go home and get some sleep to be ready for the martial arts training he had promised the boys in the morning.

He also regretted that he had not been there when AJ had

arrived after school yesterday. It had officially been the last time he was to report to him. According to McKade, AJ had come alone and had been on time. He had also done the assignment Dare had left for him to do without having much to say. However, McKade had said AJ questioned him a couple of times as to why he wasn't there.

Dare walked around the shop, wondering just what kind of flowers Shelly would like, then decided on roses. According to Storm, roses, especially red ones, said everything. And everyone knew that Storm was an ace when it came to wooing women.

"Have you decided on what you want, Sheriff?"

He turned toward Mrs. Coleman. A woman in her early sixties, she attended the same church as his parents and he'd known her all of his life. "Yes, I'd like a dozen roses."

"All right. What color?"

"Red."

She smiled and nodded as if his selection was a good one, so evidently Storm was right. "Any particular type vase you have in mind?"

He shrugged. "I haven't thought about that."

"Well, you might want to. The flowers say one thing and the vase says another. You want to make sure you select something worthy of holding your flowers."

Dare frowned. He hadn't thought ordering flowers would be so much trouble. "Do you have a selection I can take a look at?"

"Certainly. There's an entire group over on that back wall. If you see something that catches your fancy, bring it to me."

Dare nodded again. Knowing she was watching him with those keen eyes of hers, he crossed the room to stand in front of a shelf containing different vases. As far as he was concerned one vase was just as good as any, but he decided to try and look at them from a woman's point of view.

A woman like Shelly would like something that looked special, soft yet colorful. His gaze immediately went to a white ceramic vase that had flowers of different colors painted at the top. For some reason he immediately liked it and could see the dozen roses arranged really prettily in it. Without dallying any further, he picked up his choice and walked back over to the counter.

"This is the one I want."

Luanne Coleman nodded. "This is beautiful, and I'm sure she'll love it. Now, to whom will this be delivered?"

Dare inwardly smiled, knowing she was just itching to bits to know that piece of information. "Shelly Brockman."

Her brows lifted. "Shelly? Yes, I heard she was back in town, and it doesn't surprise me any that you would be hot on her heels, Dare Westmoreland. I hope you know that I was really upset with you when you broke things off with her all those years ago."

You and everybody else in this town, Dare thought, leaning against the counter.

"And she was such nice girl," Luanne continued. "And everyone knew she was so much in love with you. Poor thing had to leave town after that and her parents left not long after she did."

As Luanne accepted his charge card she glanced at him and said, "I understand she has a son."

Dare pretended not to find her subject of conversation much to his interest. He began fidgeting with several key rings she had on display. "Yes, she does."

"Someone said he's about eight or nine."

Dare knew nobody had said any such thing. The woman was fishing, and he knew it. He might as well set himself up to get caught. "He's ten."

"Ten?"

"Yes." Like you didn't already know.

"That would mean he was born soon after she left here, wouldn't it?"

Dare smiled. He liked how this woman's mind worked. "Yes, it would seem that way."

"Any ideas about his father?"

"No."

"No?"

Dare wanted to chuckle. "None."

She frowned at him. "Aren't you curious?"

"No. What Shelly did with her life after she left here is none of my business."

Dare couldn't help but notice that Luanne's frown deepened. She handed his charge card back to him and said, "I have Shelly's address, Sheriff, since she's staying at her parents' old place."

Dare nodded, not surprised that she knew that. "When will the flowers be delivered?"

"Within a few hours. Will that be soon enough?"

"Yes."

"Sheriff, can I offer you a few words of advice?"

He wondered what she would do if he said no. She would probably give him the advice anyway. He could tell she was just that upset with him right now. "Why sure, Ms. Luanne. What words of advice would you like to offer me?"

She met his gaze without blinking. "Get your head out of the sand and stop overlooking the obvious."

"Meaning?"

She frowned. "That's for you to figure out."

Shelly looked at Mr. Coleman in surprise. She then looked at the beautiful arrangement of flowers he held in his hand. "Are you sure these are for me?"

The older man beamed. "Yes, I'm positive. Luanne said

for me to get them to you right away," he said handing them to her.

"Thanks, and if you just wait a few minutes I'd like to give you a tip."

Mr. Coleman waved his hand as he went down the steps. "No need. I've already been tipped real nice for delivering them," he said with a grin that said he had a secret that he wouldn't be sharing with her.

"All right. Thanks, Mr. Coleman." She watched as he climbed into his van and drove off. Closing the door she went into the living room and placed the flowers on the first table she came to. Someone had sent her a dozen of the most beautiful red roses that she had ever seen. And the vase they were in was simply gorgeous; she could tell the vase alone had cost a pretty penny.

She quickly pulled off the card and read it aloud. "You're in my thoughts. Dare."

Her heart skipped a beat as she lightly ran her fingers over the card. Even the card and envelope weren't the standard kind that you received with a floral arrangement. They had a rich, glossy finish that caused Dare's bold signature to stand out even more.

For a moment, Shelly could only stare at the roses, the vase they were in and the card and envelope. It was obvious that a lot of time and attention had gone into their selection, and a part of her quivered inside that Dare would do something that special for her.

You're in my thoughts.

She suddenly felt tears sting her eyes. She didn't know what was wrong with her. It seemed that lately her emotions were wired and would go off at the least little thing. Ever since that day of Dare's visit and what he'd done to her on the porch, not to mention that little episode he'd orchestrated at the restaurant, she'd been battling the worst kind of drama inside her body. He had done more than open Pandora's box. He had opened a cookie jar that had been kept closed for ten years, and now she wanted Dare in the worst possible way.

"Who sent the flowers, Mom?"

Shelly lifted her head and met her son's gaze. "Your father."

He shrugged. "The sheriff?"

"One and the same." She glanced back over at the flowers. "Aren't they beautiful?"

AJ came to stand next to her. It was obvious they couldn't see the arrangement through the same eyes when he said. "Looks like a bunch of flowers to me."

She couldn't help but laugh. "Well, I think they're special, and it was thoughtful for him to send them to let me know I was in his thoughts."

AJ shrugged again. "He's looking for a girlfriend, but I told him you weren't interested in a boyfriend."

Shelly arched a brow. "AJ, you had no right to say that."

His chin jutted out. "Why not? You've never had a boyfriend before, so why would you care about one now? It's just been me and you, Mom. Isn't that enough?"

Shelly shook her head. Her son had years to learn about human sexuality and how it worked. She was just finding out herself what ten years of abstinence could do to a person. "AJ, don't you think I can get lonely sometimes?" she asked him softly.

He didn't say anything for a little while. Then he said. "But you never got lonely before."

"Yes, and I worked a lot before. That's how you got into all that trouble. I was putting in extra hours at the hospital when the cost of living got high. I needed additional money so the two of us could afford to live in the better part of town. I didn't have time to get lonely. Now with my new job, I can basically make my own hours so I can spend more time with you. But you're away in school a lot during the days, and pretty soon you'll have friends you'll want to spend time with, won't you?"

AJ thought of Morris and Cornelius and the fun they'd had on the playground that day at school. "Yes."

"Well, don't you think I need friends, too?"

"Yes, but what's wrong with having girlfriends?"

"There's nothing wrong with it, but most of the girls I went to school with have moved away, and although I'm sure I'll meet others, right now I feel comfortable associating with people I already know, like Dare and his brothers."

"But it's the sheriff who wants you as his girlfriend. He likes you."

She smiled. Dare must have laid it on rather thick. "You think so?"

"Yes. He said you used to be his special girl. His brothers and parents said so, too. And I've got a feeling he wants you to be his special girl again. But if you let him, he'll find out about me."

"And you still see that as a bad thing, AJ?"

He remained silent for a long time, then he hunched his shoulders. "I'm still not sure he would want me."

Shelly felt a knot forming in her stomach. She wondered if he was using his supposed dislike of Dare as an excuse to shield himself from getting hurt. "And why wouldn't he want you?"

"I told you that he didn't like me."

And you also said you didn't like him, she wanted to remind him, but decided to keep quiet about that. "Well, I know Dare, and I know that he likes you. He wouldn't have invited you to dinner with him and his family if he didn't. He would have taken you straight to Ms. Kate's house knowing she would have fed you."

She watched AJ's shoulders relax. "You think so?"

If you only knew, she thought. "Yes, I think so. I believe you remind Dare of himself when he was your age. I heard he was a handful for his parents. All the brothers were."

AJ nodded. "Yes, he said that once. He has a nice family."

She smiled. "Yes, he has."

AJ stuck his hands inside his pockets. "So, he's back now?"

"Who?"

"The sheriff. He left town to help another sheriff catch a guy who escaped from jail. Deputy McKade said so."

"Oh." Shelly had wondered why she hadn't heard from him since the luncheon on Thursday. Not that she had been looking for him, mind you. "Well, in that case, yes, I would say that he's back, since he ordered these flowers."

"Then our lessons for tomorrow morning are still on."

"Your lessons?"

"Yeah, remember, I told you he had said he would teach me, Morris and Cornelius how to protect ourselves at the police station in the morning."

"Oh, I'd almost forgotten about that." She wanted to meet her son's new playmates and ask Dare about them. "Will they need a ride or will their parents bring them?"

"Their parents will be bringing them. They have to go to the barbershop in the morning."

Shelly nodded, looking at the long hair on her son's head. She'd allowed him to wear it in twists, as long as they were neat-looking. Maybe in time she would suggest that he pay a visit to the barbershop as well.

"And after our class they have to go to church for choir practice."

AJ's words recaptured Shelly's attention. Morris and Cornelius were active in church? The two were sounding better and better every minute. "All right then. Go get cleaned up for dinner."

He nodded. "Do you think the sheriff will call tonight or come by?" AJ asked as he trotted up the stairs.

I wish. "I'm not sure. If he just got back into town he's probably, tired so I doubt it."

"Oh."

Although she was sure he hadn't wanted her to, she had heard the disappointment in his voice anyway. He sounded just how she felt.

Dare couldn't sleep. He felt restless. Agitated. Horny.

He threw back the covers and got out of bed, yanked a T-shirt over his head and pulled on his jeans. His body was a nagging ache, it was throbbing relentlessly and his arousal strained painfully against his jeans. He knew what his problems was, and he knew just how he could fix it.

He sighed deeply, thinking he definitely had a problem, and wondered if at two in the morning, Shelly was willing to help him solve it.

Shelly couldn't sleep and heard the sound of a pebble the moment it hit her window. At first she'd thought she was hearing things, but when a second pebble hit the window she knew she wasn't. She also knew who was sending her the signals to come to the backyard.

That had always been Dare's secret sign to let her know he was back in town. She would then sneak past her parents' bedroom and slip down the stairs and through the back door to race outside to his arms.

She immediately got out of bed, tugged on her robe and slipped her feet into her slippers. Not even thinking about why he would be outside her window this time of night, she quickly tiptoed down the stairs. Without turning on a light, she entered the kitchen and opened the back door, and, although it was too dark for her to see, she knew he was there. Her nostrils immediately picked up his scent.

"Dare?" she whispered, squinting her eyes to see him.

"I'm here."

And he was, suddenly looming over her, gazing down at her with a look in his eyes that couldn't be disguised. It was desperate, hot, intense, and it made her own eyes sizzle at the same time the area between her legs began to throb. "I heard the pebbles," she said, swallowing deeply.

He nodded as he continued to hold her gaze. "I was hoping you would remember what it meant."

Oh, she remembered all right. Her body remembered, too. "Why are you here?" she asked softly, feeling her insides heat up and an incredible sensation flow between her legs. Desire was surging through every part of her body and she was barely able to stand it. "What do you want, Dare?"

He reached out and placed both hands at her waist, intentionally pulling her closer so she could feel his large, hard erection straining against his jeans. "I think that's a big indication of what I want, Shelly," he murmured huskily, leaning down as his mouth drew closer to hers.

Ten

Shelly felt a moment of panic. One part of her mind tried telling her that she didn't want this, but another part, the one ruled by her body, quickly convinced her that she did. Her mind was swamped with the belief that it didn't matter that it hadn't been a full week since she laid eyes on Dare again after ten years. Nor did it matter that there were issues yet unresolved between them. The only thing that mattered was that this was the man she had once loved to distraction, the man she had given her virginity to at seventeen; the man who had taught her all the pleasures a man and woman could share, and the man who had given her a son. And, she inwardly told herself, this has nothing to do with love but with gratifying our needs.

Realizing that and accepting it, her body trembled as she lifted her face to meet his, and at that moment everything, including the ten years that had separated them, evaporated and was replaced by hunger, intense, sexual hunger that was waiting to explode within her. He felt it too, and his body reacted, drawing her closer and making a groan escape from her lips.

He covered her mouth with his, zapping her senses in a way that only he could do. Fueled by the greed they both felt, his kiss wasn't gentle. It displayed all the insatiability he was feeling.

And then some.

Dare didn't think he could get enough. He wanted to get inside her, reacquaint her body with his and give her the satisfaction she had denied herself for ten years. He wanted to give her *him*. He felt his blood boil as he pulled his mouth from hers with a labored breath. She was shaking almost violently. So was he.

"Come with me. I've got a place set up for us."

Nodding, she let him lead her off the back porch and through a thicket of trees to a spot hidden by low overhanging branches, a place they had once considered theirs. It was dark, but she was able to make out the blanket that had been spread on the ground. As always, he had thought ahead. He had planned her seduction well this night.

"Where did you park your car?" she asked wondering how he had managed things.

"At the station. I walked from there, using the back way. And nobody saw me."

She nodded. Evidently he had read her mind. From the information she had gotten from Ms. Kate earlier today, the town was buzzing about AJ, wondering if Dare was actually too dim-witted to figure out her son was his.

She met his gaze, which was illuminated by the moonlight. "Thanks for the flowers. They're beautiful. You didn't have to send them."

"I wanted to send them, Shelly."

He drew in a deep breath, and she saw that his gaze was

glued to her mouth just as hers was glued to his. She couldn't help but think of the way he tasted, the hunger and intense desire that was still blatant in his loins, making his erection even bigger. Their need for each other had never been this sharp, all-consuming.

"I want you, Shelly," he whispered gently, pulling her down to the blanket with him.

She went willingly, without any resistance, letting him know that she wanted the intimacy of this night as much as he did. She wanted to lose herself in him in the same way he wanted to lose himself in her. Totally. Completely.

She didn't say a word as he gently pushed her robe from her shoulders, and then pulled her nightgown over her head. Nor did she utter a sound when his fingers caressed her breasts then tweaked her nipples before moving lower, past her rib cage and her stomach until he reached the area between her legs.

When he touched her there, dipped into her warmth, her breathing quickened and strained and she almost cried out.

"You're so wet," his voice rumbled against her lips. "All I could think about over the last couple of days is devouring you, wanting the taste of you on my tongue.

Heat built within her body as he pushed her even more over the edge, making her whimper in pleasure. And when pleasure erupted inside her with the force of a tidal wave, he was there to intensify it.

He kissed the scream of his name from her lips, again taking control of her mouth. The kiss was sensual, the taste erotic and it fueled her fire even more. She had ten years to make up for, and somehow, she knew, he was well aware of that.

When her body ceased its trembling, he pulled back, ending their kiss, and stood to remove his clothes. She looked up at him as he tossed his T-shirt aside. He appeared cool and in control as he undressed in front of her, but she knew he was not. His gaze was on her, and she again she connected with it. It felt like a hot caress.

She watched as he eased down his jeans, and she gasped. Her mouth became moist, her body got hungrier. He wasn't wearing any underwear and his erection sprang forth—full of life, eager to please and ready to go. The tip seemed to point straight at her, and the only thing she could think about was the gigantic orgasm she knew Dare would give her.

Anticipation surged within her when he kicked his jeans aside and stood before her completely naked. And her senses began overflowing with the scent of an aroused man.

An aroused man who was ready to mate with an aroused woman.

She then noticed the condom packet he held in his hand. It seemed he had planned her seduction down to the last detail. She watched as he readied himself to keep her safe. Inhaling deeply when the task was done, he lifted his head and met her gaze.

"This is where you tell me to stop, Shelly, and I will."

She knew him, trusted him and realized that what he'd said was true. No matter how much he wanted her, he would never force himself on her. But then, he need not worry about her turning him down. Her body was on fire for him, the area between her legs throbbed. He had given her relief earlier, but that hadn't been enough. She wanted the same thing he wanted.

Deep penetration.

They had discovered a long time ago that they were two intensely sexual human beings. Anytime he had wanted her, all he had to do was touch her and he would have her hot, wet and pulsing within minutes. And anytime they mated, neither had control other than to make sure she was protected from pregnancy, except for that one time when they hadn't even had control for that.

When he dropped down to rejoin her on the blanket, she drew in a deep breath and automatically wrapped her arms around him as he poised his body over hers. He leaned down and placed a kiss on her lips.

"Thank you for my son."

A groan gently left her throat when she felt the head of him pressed against her entrance. Hot and swollen. He nudged her legs apart a little wider with his knees as his gaze continued to hold hers. "Ten years of missing you and not sharing this, Shelly."

And then he entered her, slowly, methodically, trembling as his body continued to push into hers as he lifted her hips. He let out a deep guttural moan. In no time at all he was planted within her to the hilt. The muscles of her body were clenching him. Milking him. Reclaiming him.

She held his gaze and when he smiled, so did she.

And then he began an easy rhythm. Slowly, painstakingly, he increased the pace. And with each deep thrust, he reminded her of just how things used to be between them, and how things still were now.

Hungry. Intense. Overpowering.

His gaze became keen, concentrated and potently dark each time he thrust forward, drove deeper into her, and she felt her body dissolve, dissipate then fuse into his. She felt the muscles of his shoulders bunch beneath her hands, heard the masculine sound of his growl and knew he was fighting reaching sexual fulfillment, waiting for her, refusing to leave her behind. But he couldn't hold back any longer, and, with one last, hard, deep thrust his body began shaking as he reached the pinnacle of satisfaction.

His orgasm triggered hers, and when her mouth formed a chilling scream, he quickly covered it with his, denying her the chance to wake the entire neighborhood. But he couldn't stop her body from quivering uncontrollably. Nor could he stop her legs from wrapping around him, locking their bodies together, determined that they continue to share this. She closed her eyes as a feeling of unspeakable joy and gratification claimed her in the most provocative way, restitution, compensation for ten years of not having access to any of this.

And when the last of the shudders subsided and they both continued to shiver in the aftermath, he sank down, lowered his head to the curve of her neck, released a deep satisfied sigh, and wondered what words he could say to let her know just how overwhelmed he felt.

He forced himself to lift up, to meet her gaze, and she opened her eyes and looked at him. And at that moment, in that instant, he knew words weren't needed. There was no way she couldn't know how he felt.

And as he leaned down and kissed her, he knew that the rest of the night belonged to them.

"Mom? Mom? Are you all right?"

Shelly opened her eyes as she felt AJ nudge her awake. Once again he had found her sleeping on the sofa. After several more bouts of intense lovemaking, they had re-dressed, then Dare had gathered her into his arms and carried her inside the house. Not wanting to risk taking her upstairs to her own bed and running into AJ, just in case he had awakened during the night to use the bathroom or something, she had asked Dare to place her on the sofa.

Now she turned over to meet AJ's gaze and felt the soreness between her legs as she did so. She had used muscles last night that she hadn't used in over ten years. "Yes, sweetheart, I'm fine."

He lifted a brow. "You slept on the sofa again."

She glanced at the book that was still where it had been the last time she had used it for an alibi. "I guess I fell asleep reading again." She glanced at the clock on the wall. It was Saturday which meant it wasn't a school day so why was he up so early? "Isn't this your day to sleep late?"

He smiled sheepishly, and that smile reminded her so much of Dare that her breath almost caught. "Yeah, but the sheriff is giving us martial arts lessons today, remember?"

Yes, she remembered, then she wondered if after last night Dare would be in any physical shape to give the boys anything today. But then he was a man, and men recovered from intense sessions of lovemaking a lot quicker than most women. Besides, she doubted if he'd gone without sex for ten years as she had. She forced the thought from her mind, not wanting to think about Dare making love to other women.

She shifted her attention back to AJ. "You're excited about taking lessons from Dare aren't you?"

He shrugged. "Yes, I guess. I've always wanted to learn some type of martial arts, but you never would let me take any classes. Morris said his father told him that the sheriff is an ace when it comes to that sort of stuff, and I'm hoping he'll be willing to give us more than one lesson."

Shelly wondered if AJ would ever stop referring to Dare as "the sheriff." But then, to call him Dare was even less respectful. "All right, do you want pancakes this morning?"

"Yes! With lots and lots of butter!"

She smiled as she stood, wincing in the process. Her sore muscles definitely reminded her of last night. "Not with lots and lots of butter, AJ, but I'll make sure you get enough."

Shelly saw Dare the moment she pulled her car into the parking lot at the sheriff's office. He walked over to the car and met them. She wasn't surprised to discover that he'd been waiting for them.

"Are we late?" AJ asked quickly, meeting Dare's gaze.

Dare smiled at him. "No, Cornelius isn't here yet, but I understand he's on his way. Morris's mother just dropped him off a few minutes ago. He's waiting inside."

He then looked at Shelly, and his smile widened. "And how are you doing this morning, Shelly?"

She returned his smile, thinking about all the things the two of them had done last night while most of College Park slept. "I'm fine, Dare, what about you?"

"This is the best I've felt in years." He wanted to say ten years to be exact, but didn't want AJ to catch on to anything.

Shelly glanced at her watch. "How long will the lessons last today?"

"At least an hour or so. Why? Is there something you need to do?"

Shelly placed an arm around AJ's shoulders. "Well, I was hoping I'd have enough time to get my nails done in addition to getting my hair taken care of."

"Then do it. I'm going over to Thorn's shop when I leave here to check out the new bike that he's building. AJ is welcome to go with me if he likes and I can bring him home later."

He shifted his glance from Shelly to AJ. "Would you like to go to Thorn's shop to see how he puts a motorcycle together?"

The expression in AJ's eyes told Dare that he would. "Yes, I'd love to go!" He turned to Shelly. "Can I, Mom?"

Shelly met Dare's gaze. "Are you sure, Dare? I wouldn't want to put you out with having to—"

"No, I'd like his company."

AJ's eyes widened in surprise. "You would?"

Dare grinned. "Sure, I would. You did a great job with

all the chores that I assigned to you this week, and I doubt that you'll be playing hooky from school anytime soon, right?"

AJ lowered his head to study his sneakers. "Right."

"Then that does it. My brothers will be there and I know for a fact they'd like to see you again."

AJ smiled. "They would?"

"Yes, they would. They said they enjoyed having you at dinner the other night. Usually on Saturday we all pitch in to give Thorn a hand to make sure any bike he's building is ready to be delivered on time. The one he's working on now is for Sylvester Stallone."

"Wow!"

Dare laughed at the astonishment he heard in AJ's voice and the look of awe on his face. What he'd said about his brothers wanting to see AJ again was true. They were biting at the bit for a chance to spend more time with their nephew.

"Well, I guess that's settled," Shelly said, smiling at Dare and the son he had given her. "I'd better get going if I want to make my hair appointment on time." She turned to leave.

"Shelly?"

She turned back around. "Yes?"

"I almost forgot to mention that Mom called this morning. She heard from Laney last night. She, Jamal and the baby are coming for a visit in a couple of weeks and will stay for about two months. Then they will be moving to stay at their place in Bowling Green, Kentucky while Laney completes her residency at the hospital there."

Shelly smiled. When she'd last seen Dare's baby sister, Delaney was just about to turn sixteen and the brothers were having a time keeping the young men away. Now she had graduated from medical school and had landed herself a prince from the Middle East. She was a princess and the mother to a son who would one day grow up to be a king. "That's wonderful! I can't wait to see her again."

Dare grinned. "And she can't wait to see you, either. Mom told her that you had moved back and she was excited about it."

Without having to worry about AJ, Shelly decided to throw in a pedicure after getting her hair and nails done. Upon returning home, she collapsed on the bed and took a nap. The lack of sleep the night before still had her tired. After waking up, she was about to go outside on the porch and sit in the swing when she heard a knock at the door. She glanced through the peephole and saw it was Dare and AJ. Both of them had their hands and, faces smeared with what looked like motor oil. She frowned. If they thought they were coming inside her house looking like that, they had another thought coming.

"Go around back," she instructed, opening the door just a little ways. "I'll bring you washcloths and a scrub brush to clean up. You can also use the hose." She then quickly closed the door.

She met them in the backyard where they were using the hose to wash oil from their hair. It was then that she noticed several oil spots on AJ's outfit as well. "What on earth happened?"

"Storm happened," Dare grumbled, taking the shampoo and towel she handed him. His frown indicated he wasn't all that happy about it either. "You know how he likes to play around? Well, for some reason he decided to fill a water gun with motor oil, and AJ and I became his victims."

She shifted her gaze from Dare to AJ. Whereas Dare was not a happy camper because of Storm's childish antics, it seemed AJ was just the opposite. "Storm is so much fun!"

He said, laughing. "He told me all about how he had to save this little old lady from a burning house once."

Shelly smiled. "Well, I'm glad you enjoyed yourself, but those clothes can stay out here. In fact, we may as well trash them."

AJ nodded. "Storm said to tell you that he's going to buy me another outfit and he'll call to find out when he can take me shopping."

Shelly crossed her arms over her chest and lifted a brow. "Oh, he did, did he?"

"Yes."

She shifted her gaze back to Dare. "What are we going to do about that brother of yours?"

Dare shrugged, smiling. "What can I do? I guess we could try marrying him off, except so far there's not a woman around who suits his fancy except for Tara, but she's Thorn's challenge."

A bemused look covered Shelly face. "What?"

"Tara Matthews. She's Laney's friend—a doctor who works at the same hospital in Kentucky where Delaney plans to complete her residency. I'll explain about her being Thorn's challenge at another time."

Shelly nodded, planning to hold him to that. She glanced down at her watch. "I was about to cook burgers and fries, if anyone is interested."

Dare looked pleased. "Only if you let me grill the burgers."

"And I'll help," AJ chimed in, volunteering his services.

Shelly shook her head. "All right, and I'll cook the fries and make some potato salad and baked beans to go along with it. How does that sound?"

"That sounds great, Mom."

Shelly nodded, liking the excitement she heard in her son's voice. "Dare?"

He chuckled. "I agree with AJ. That sounds great."

Dare remained through dinner. He got a call that he had to take care of, but returned later with Chase and Storm close on his heels. They brought a checkers game, intent on showing AJ how to play. It was almost eleven before AJ finally admitted he was too tired to play another game. Chase and Storm left after AJ went to bed, leaving Dare to follow later after they mentioned they were headed over to Thorn's place to wake him up to play a game of poker.

An hour or so later, Shelly walked Dare to the door. He had spent some time telling her how Tara Matthews was a feisty woman that only Thorn could tame and that was why the brothers referred to her as Thorn's challenge. "So you think this Tara Matthews has captured the eye of Thorn Westmoreland?"

Dare chuckled. "Yes, although he doesn't know it yet, and I feel sorry for Tara when he does."

Shelly nodded. Moments later she said. "I hope you know your leaving late is giving the neighbors a lot to say."

He smiled. "Yeah, I heard from McKade that a lot of people around town are questioning my intelligence. They think I haven't figured out that AJ's my son."

Shelly nodded. "Yes, that's what I'm hearing, too, from Ms. Kate."

"How do you think AJ is handling things?"

"I don't think anyone has said anything to him directly, but I know a couple of people have asked him about his father in a roundabout way."

Dare lifted a brow. "When?"

"A couple of days ago at Kate's Diner. He goes there every morning on his way to school."

Dare nodded. "Damn, Shelly, I'm ready to end this farce and let this whole damn town know AJ's mine."

"I know, Dare, but remember we decided to let him be the one to determine when that would be. Personally, I think it'll be sooner than you think, because he's slowly coming around."

Dare raised a questioning brow. "You think so?"

"Yes. The two of you are interacting together a lot better. That's obvious. I can tell, and I know your brothers picked up on it tonight as well."

"Yes, but for some reason he still holds himself back from me," Dare said in a frustrated tone. "I sense it, Shelly, and it bothers the heck out of me. I don't know why he's doing it."

Shelly smiled slightly. "I think I do."

Dare met her gaze. "Then tell me—why?"

She sighed. "I think AJ is beginning to wonder if he's good enough to be your son."

Dare frowned. "Why would he wonder about a thing like that?"

"Because basically he's beginning to see you through a new set of eyes, the same eyes Morris and Cornelius see you with, and AJ's concerned about the way the two of you met. He knows it wasn't a good start and that you were disappointed with him. Now he's afraid that he won't be able to wipe the slate clean with you."

Dare rubbed a hand down his face. "There'll never be a time that I wouldn't want my son, Shelly."

She wrapped her arms around his waist upon hearing the frustration in his voice. She heard the love there as well. "I know that and you know that, but he has to know that, too. Now that you've broken the ice with him, it's time for you to get to know him and for him to get to know you. Then he'll see that no matter what, you'll always be there for him."

Dare let out a deep sigh. "And I thought winning him over would be easy."

She smiled. "In a way, it has been. To be honest with you, I really didn't expect him to come around this soon. Like you, he has somewhat of a stubborn streak about certain things. Him coming around the way he has just goes to show that you evidently have a way with people."

Dare smiled and brought her closer to him. "And do I have a way with you, Shelly?" The only reason he wasn't making love to her again tonight was that he was well aware of the fact that her body was sore. He couldn't help noticing how stiff her movements were when she'd dropped AJ off that morning and again this evening at dinner.

"After last night how can you even ask that, Dare? You know I was putty in your hands," she said, recapturing his attention.

"Then that makes us even, because I was definitely putty in yours as well." He leaned down and kissed her, thinking of just how right she felt in his arms.

Just like always.

Eleven

Shelly stretched out in her bed with a sensuous sigh. Almost two weeks had passed since she and Dare had spent the night together on a blanket in her backyard. Since then, nightly meetings in the backyard on a blanket had become almost a ritual. He had become almost a fixture in her home, dropping by for dinner, and inviting her and AJ to a movie or some other function in town.

AJ was beginning to let his guard down around Dare, but as yet he had not acknowledged him as his father. Shelly knew Dare's patience was wearing thin; he was eager to claim his son, but as she had explained to Dare weeks ago, AJ had to believe in his heart that his father wanted him for a son before he could give Dare his complete love and trust.

She then thought about her own feelings for Dare. She had to fight hard to keep from falling in love with Dare all over again. She had to remember they were playacting for

AJ's sake. To anyone observing them, it seemed that he was wooing her. He was giving the towns people something to talk about with the different flower arrangements that he sent her each week.

A couple of people had taken her aside and warned her not to be setting herself up for heartbreak all over again, since everyone knew Dare Westmoreland was a staunch bachelor. But there were others who truly felt he was worthy of another chance, and they tried convincing her that if anyone could change Dare's bachelor status, she could.

What she couldn't tell them was that she was not interested in changing Dare's bachelor status. Although she had detected some changes in him, she could not forget that at one time he had been a man driven to reach out for dreams that had not included her. And she could never let herself become vulnerable to that type of pain again. For six years she had believed she was the most important thing in Dare's life, and to find out that she hadn't been had nearly destroyed her. She had enough common sense to know that what she and Dare were sharing in the backyard at night was not based on emotional but on physical needs, and as long as she was able to continue to know the difference, she would be all right.

She pulled herself up in bed when she heard the knock on her bedroom door. "Come in, AJ."

It was early still, an hour before daybreak, but she knew he was excited. Today was the day that Dare's sister Delaney and her family were arriving from the Middle East. The Westmoreland brothers were ecstatic and had talked about their one and only sister so much over the past two weeks that AJ had gotten caught up in their excitement; after all, the woman was his aunt, although he assumed Delaney didn't know it.

He opened the door and stood just within the shadows

of the light coming in from the hallway. Again, Shelly couldn't help but notice just how much he looked like Dare. No wonder the town was buzzing. "What is it, AJ?"

He shrugged. "I wanted to talk to you about something, Mom."

She nodded and scooted over in bed, but he went and sat in the chair. Evidently, he thought he was past the age to get into his mother's bed. Shelly's heart caught. Her son was becoming a young man and with his budding maturity came a lot of issues that Dare would be there to help her with. Not only Dare but the entire Westmoreland family.

He remained silent for a few minutes, then he spoke. "I've decided to tell the sheriff I'm his son."

Shelly's heart did a flip, and she swallowed slowly. "When did you decide that?"

"Yesterday."

"And what made you change your mind?"

"I've been watching him, Mom. I was in Kate's Diner one morning last week when he came in, but he didn't see me at first. When he walked in, all the people there acted like they were glad to see him, and he knew all their names and asked them how they were doing. Then it hit me that he really wasn't a bad cop or a mean cop at all. No one would like him if he was, and everybody likes him, Mom."

Shelly blinked away the tears from her eyes. AJ was right. Everyone liked Dare and thought well of him. AJ had had to discover that on his own, and it seemed that he had. "Yes, everyone likes Dare. He's a good sheriff and he's fair, AJ."

"Most of the kids at school thinks he's the bomb and feel that I'm lucky because you're his girlfriend."

Shelly made a surprised face. "The kids at your school think I'm his girlfriend?"

AJ nodded. "Well, aren't you?"

Shelly smiled slightly. She didn't want to give him hope

that things would work out between her and Dare, and that once he admitted to being Dare's son they would miraculously become a loving family. "No, AJ, although we're close, Dare and I are nothing more than good friends. We always have been and always will be."

"But he wants you for his girlfriend, I can tell. Everyone can tell and they're all talking about it, as well as the fact they think I'm his son, although they don't want me to hear that part, but I do. The sheriff spends a lot of time with us and takes us places with him. The kids at school say their parents think it's time for him to settle down and marry, and I can tell that he really likes you, Mom. He always treats you special and I like that."

Shelly inhaled deeply. She liked it, too, but she knew a lot more about why Dare was spending time with her than AJ did. It was all part of his plan to gain his son's love and trust. She refused to put too much stock into anything else, not even the many times they had slept together. She knew it had to do with their raging hormones and nothing more. "So, when are you going to tell him?" she asked quietly.

AJ shrugged. "I still don't know that yet. But I wanted to let you know that I would be telling him."

She nodded. "Don't take too long. Like I said, Dare won't be a happy camper knowing we kept it from him, but I believe he'll be so happy about you that he'll quickly come around."

AJ's eyes lit up. "You think so?"

"Yes, sweetheart, I do."

He nodded. "Then I might tell him today. He asked if I'd like to go with him to meet his sister and her family at the airport. I might tell him then."

Shelly nodded again, knowing that if he did, it would certainly make Dare's day.

AJ thought Dare's truck was really cool. He had ridden in it a couple of times before, and just like the other times, he thought it was a nice vehicle for a sheriff to have when you wanted to stop being sheriff for a little while. But as he looked at Dare out of the corner of his eyes, he knew that the sheriff was always the sheriff. There was probably never a time he when he wasn't on the job, and that included times like now when he wasn't wearing his uniform.

"So are you looking forward to that day out of school next Friday for teachers' planning day?" Dare asked the moment he'd made sure AJ had snapped his seatbelt in place. Once that was done, he started the engine.

"Yes, although Mom will probably find a lot of work for me to do that day." He didn't say anything else for a little while, then he asked quickly, "Do you like kids?"

Dare glanced over at him and smiled. "Yes, I like kids."

"Do you ever plan to have any?"

Dare lifted his brow. "Yeah, one day. Why do you ask?"

AJ shrugged. "No reason."

Dare checked the rearview mirror as he began backing out of Shelly's driveway. He was headed for the airport like the rest of his family to welcome his sister home. He couldn't help wondering if AJ had started quizzing him for some reason and inwardly smiled, ready for any questions that his son felt he needed to ask.

Princess Delaney Westmoreland Yasir clutched her son to her breast and inhaled sharply. She leaned against her husband's side for support. Her mother had said Shelly's son favored Dare, but what she was seeing was uncanny. There was no way anyone could take a look at the boy standing next to Dare and not immediately know they were father and son. They had the same coffee coloring, the same dark intense eyes and the same shape mouth and nose. AJ Brockman was a little Dare; a small replica of his father, there was no doubt of that.

"And who do we have here?" She asked after regaining her composure and giving her parents and brothers hugs.

"This is AJ," Dare said meeting his sister's astonished gaze. "Shelly Brockman's son. I think Mom mentioned to you that she had returned to town."

Delaney nodded. "Yes, that's what I heard." She smiled down at AJ and immediately fell in love. He was a Westmoreland, and she was happy to claim him. "And how are you, AJ?" she asked her nephew, offering him her hand.

"I'm fine, thank you," he said somewhat shyly.

"And how is your mother?"

"She's doing fine. She said she couldn't wait to see you later today."

Delaney smiled. "And I can't wait to see her. She was like a big sister to me."

With love shining in her eyes, Delaney then glanced at the imposing figure at her side and smiled. "AJ, this is my husband, Jamal Ari Yasir."

AJ switched his gaze from Delaney to the tall man standing next to her. He wasn't sure what he should do. Was he supposed to bow or something? He let out a deep sigh of relief when the man stooped down to his level and met his gaze. "And how are you, AJ?" he asked in a deep voice, smiling.

AJ couldn't help but return the man's smile, suddenly feeling at ease. "I'm fine, sir."

When the man straightened back up, AJ switched his gaze to the baby Delaney held in her arms. "May I see him?"

Delaney beamed. "Sure. His name is Ari Terek Yasir." She leaned down and uncovered her son for AJ to see. The baby glanced at AJ and smiled. AJ smiled back, and so did everyone else standing around them at the airport. Delaney looked over at her mother, in whose eyes tears of happiness shone at seeing her two grandsons together getting acquainted.

Suddenly Prince Jamal Ari Yasir cleared his throat. Everyone had become misty-eyed and silent, and he decided to put the spark and excitement back into the welcome gathering. This was the family he had come to love, thanks to his wife who he truly cherished. His dark eyes shone with amusement as he addressed the one brother who he hadn't completely won over yet. "So, Thorn, are you still being a thorn in everyone's side these days?" he asked smiling.

Twelve

Shelly smiled as she looked at the young woman sitting in the chair across from her on the patio at Dare's parents' home. The last time she had seen Delaney Westmoreland she'd been a teenager, a few months shy of her sixteenth birthday, a rebellious, feisty opponent who'd been trying to stand up to her five overprotective and oftentimes overbearing brothers.

Now she was a self-assured, confident young woman, a medical doctor, mother to a beautiful baby boy and wife to a gorgeous sheikh from a country in the Middle East called Tahran. And from the looks the prince was constantly giving his wife, there was no doubt in her mind that Delaney was also a woman well loved and desired.

And, Shelly thought further, Delaney was breathtakingly stunning. Even all those years back there had never been any doubt in Shelly's mind that Delaney would grow up to become a beauty. She was sure there hadn't been any doubt in the brothers' minds of that as well, which was probably the reason they had tried keeping such a tight rein on her. But clearly they had not been a match for Prince Jamal Ari Yasir.

Delaney and Shelly were alone on the patio. Mrs. Westmoreland was inside, singing Ari to sleep, and AJ had gone with his father and grandfather to the store to buy more charcoal. The brothers and Jamal had taken a quick run to Thorn's shop for Jamal to take a look at Thorn's latest beauty of a bike.

"I'm glad you returned, Shelly, to bring AJ home to Dare and to us. I don't think you know how happy you've made my parents. They thought Ari was their only grandchild and were fretting over the fact they wouldn't be able to see him as often as they wanted to. I felt awful about that, but knew my place was with Jamal, which meant living in his country the majority of the time. One good thing is that as long as his father is king, we have the luxury of traveling as much as we want. But things will change once Jamal becomes king."

When Shelly nodded, she continued. "We hope that won't happen for a while. His father is in excellent health and has no plans to turn things over to Jamal just yet."

After a long moment of silence, Shelly said, "I want to apologize for leaving the way I did ten years ago, Delaney, and for not staying in touch."

Delaney's eyes shone in understanding. "Trust me, we all understood your need to put distance between you and Dare. Everyone got on his case after you left, and for a while there was friction between him and my brothers."

Shelly nodded. Dare had told her as much.

"Mom explained the situation to me about AJ," Delaney added, breaking into Shelly's thoughts. "She told me how you and Dare have decided to let him be the one to tell Dare the truth. What's the latest on that? Is he softening any toward Dare? As someone just arriving on the scene, I'd say they seem to be getting along just fine."

Shelly nodded, remembering AJ's intense dislike of Dare in the beginning. "I think he's discovered Dare isn't the mean cop that he thought he was, and yes, he is definitely softening. He even told me this morning that he plans to tell Dare that he's his father."

A huge smile touched Delaney's features. "When?"

"Now, that I don't know. From what I gather he'll tell Dare when they get a private moment and when he feels the time is right. He's battling his fear that Dare may not want him because of the way he behaved in the beginning."

Delaney shook her head. "There's no way Dare would not want his son."

"Yes, I know, but AJ has to realize that for himself."

Delaney nodded, knowing Shelly was right.

AJ stood next to Dare in the supermarket line. He watched as the sheriff pulled money from his wallet to pay for his purchases. When they walked outside to wait for Mr. Westmoreland, who was still inside buying a few additional items he'd discovered he needed, AJ decided to use that time to ask Dare a couple more questions.

"Can I ask you something?"

Dare looked at him. "Sure. Ask me anything you want to know, AJ."

"Earlier today you said you liked kids. If you ever marry, do you think you'd want more than one child?"

Dare wondered about the reason for that question. Was AJ contented being an only child? Would he feel threatened if Dare told him that he relished the thought of having other children—if Shelly would be their mother? He sighed, deciding to be completely honest with his son.

"Yes, I'd want more than one child. I'd like as many as my wife would agree to give me."

AJ's face remained expressionless, and Dare didn't have a clue if the answer he'd given would help him or hang him. "Any more questions?"

For a long moment, AJ didn't say anything. Then he met Dare's gaze and asked, "Is Dare your real name?"

Dare shook his head. "No, my real name is Alisdare Julian Westmoreland." He continued to hold his son's gaze. "Why do you ask?"

AJ placed his hands into his pockets. "Because my name is Alisdare Julian, too. That's what the AJ stands for."

Dare wasn't sure exactly what he was supposed to say, but knew he should act surprised, so he did. He raised his dark brows as if somewhat astonished. "Your mother named you after me?"

AJ nodded. "Yes."

Dare stared at AJ for a moment before asking. "Why did she do that?"

He watched as his son drew a deep breath. "Because—"

"Sorry I took so long. I bet your mom thinks the three of us have been kidnapped."

Both Dare and AJ turned to see Mr. Westmoreland walking toward them. But Dare was determine his son would finish what he'd been about to say. He returned his gaze to AJ. "Because—?"

AJ looked at the older man walking toward them, and then at Dare and, after losing his nerve, quickly said, "Because she liked your name."

"Because she liked your name."

Later that night Dare shook his head, remembering the reason AJ had given him for Shelly's choice of his name. He knew without a shadow of a doubt that AJ had come within a second of finally telling him he was his son before his father had unintentionally interrupted them, destroying that chance. But Dare was determined he would get it again.

Once they'd returned to his parents' home, there had been no private time, and on more than one occasion he'd been tempted to suggest that the two of them go back to the store and pick up some item his mother just had to have, but since his brothers and Jamal hadn't yet returned, his mother put him to work helping his father grill the ribs and steaks.

Now it was past eleven and Shelly was gathering her things to take a tired and sleepy AJ home. He had gotten worn out playing table tennis with his uncles for the past couple of hours.

Dare studied Shelly, as he'd been doing most of the night. She was wearing a pair of jeans that molded to her curvaceous hips and a blue pullover top that, to him, emphasized her lush breasts. Breasts he'd been kissing and tasting quite a lot over the past few weeks. Her body had always been a complete turn-on to him, and nothing had changed. He'd been fighting an arousal all night. The last thing he needed was for his brothers to detect what a bad way he was in, although from the smirks they had sent him most of the evening, he was well aware that they knew.

"AJ and I are going to have to say goodnight to everyone," Shelly said smiling. "Thanks again for inviting us." She met Dare's gaze and blinked at his unspoken message. He was letting her know that he would be seeing her later tonight.

He slowly crossed the room to her. "I'll walk the two of you out."

She nodded before turning to give Delaney and Jamal, the elder Westmorelands and finally the brothers hugs.

Dare frowned at Storm when he deliberately kissed Shelly on the lips, trying to get a rise out of him and knowing it had worked. As far as Dare was concerned Shelly was his, and he didn't appreciate anyone mauling her. He had put up with it the first time they'd seen her at Chase's restaurant, but now he figured that it was time Storm learned to keep his hands and his lips to himself.

When Shelly and AJ walked ahead of him going out the door, he hung back and growled to Storm. "If you ever do that again, I'll break your arm."

He ignored Storm's burst of laughter and followed Shelly and AJ outside.

It was a beautiful night. The air felt crisp, pleasantly cool as Shelly closed the back door behind her and raced across the backyard to the place where she knew Dare was waiting for her. She hadn't bothered to put on a robe, since he would be taking it off her anyway, and she hadn't bothered to put on a gown, preferring to slip into an oversized T-shirt instead.

It had taken her some time to get AJ settled and into bed after arriving home from the Westmorelands. They had talked; he had told her that he'd come close to telling Dare the truth tonight, but that he'd been interrupted. She knew the longer he put it off, the harder it was going to be for him.

"Shelly?"

She sucked in a deep breath when Dare emerged from the shadows, dazzling her senses beneath the glow of a full moon. She immediately walked into his arms. Dark, penetrating eyes met hers and then, in a deep, ragged breath, he tipped her head back as his lips captured hers.

The whimpered sounds erupting from deep within her throat propelled him forward, making the urge for them to mate that more intense, urgent, imperative. He gently lifted her T-shirt and touched her, discovering she was completely bare underneath. With unerring speed he lifted her off her feet, wrapped her legs around his waist and walked a few steps to a nearby tree.

She saw it was another seduction, planned down to every detail. Evidently he'd kept himself busy while waiting for her, she thought, noticing he had securely tied a huge pillow around the tree trunk. It served as a cushion for her backside when he pressed her against it. And then he was breathing hard and heavy while unzipping his pants and reaching inside to free himself. "I knew I couldn't wait, so I've already taken care of protection," he whispered as he thrust forward, entering her.

At her quick intake of breath, he covered her mouth with his, sipping the nectar of surprise from her lips, playing around in her mouth with his tongue as if relishing the taste of her. How long ago had they last kissed? Hadn't it been just last night? You couldn't tell by the way he was eating away at her mouth and the way she eagerly responded, wanting, needing and desiring him with a vengeance.

She opened he legs wider, wrapped them around his waist tighter when he went deeper, sending shock waves of pleasure racing through her. She felt close, so very close to the edge, and she knew she wanted him to be with her when she fell.

She broke off their kiss. "Now, Dare!"

Dare began moving. Throwing his head back he inhaled a deep whiff of her scent—hot, enticing, sensually hers— and totally lost it. His jaw clenched as he thrust deeper, moved faster, when she arched her back. Desperately, he mated with her with quick, precise strokes, giving her all he had and taking all she had to give.

He was past the point of no return and she was right there with him. And when he felt her body tighten and the spasm rip through her, bringing with it an orgasm so powerful that he felt the earth shake beneath his feet, he held her gaze and thrust into her one final time as he joined her in a climax that just wouldn't stop. The sensations started at the top of his head and moved downward at lightning speed, building intense pressure in that part of his body nestled deep inside her, and making him clench his teeth to keep from screaming out her name and stomping his feet.

The sensations kept coming and coming and he leaned forward to kiss her again, capturing the essence of what they were sharing. As his body continued to tremble while buried deep inside of her, he knew that even after ten long years, he was still seductively, passionately and irrevocably hers. She was the only woman he would ever want. The only woman he would ever need. The only woman who could make him understand and appreciate the difference between having mind-blowing sex and making earth-shattering, soul-stirring, deep-down-in-your-gut love.

She was the only woman.

And he also knew that she was the only woman he would ever love and that he still loved her.

Moments later, Dare pulled his body from Shelly's and, gathering her gently into his arms, walked over to place her on the blanket. He stretched out on his side facing her as he waited for the air to return back to his lungs and the blood to stop rushing fast and furious through his veins.

"I was beginning to think you weren't coming," he finally said some time later, the tone of his voice still quivering from the afterglow of what they'd just shared.

He couldn't help touching her again, so he slid his hand across her stomach, gently stroking her. He remembered the question AJ had asked him about wanting other children, and he remembered thinking that he'd want more children only if Shelly were their mother. He wouldn't hesitate putting another child of his inside her, in the womb he knew he had touched tonight. Not only had he touched it, he had branded it his.

Shelly slowly opened her eyes as her world settled, and the explosion she'd felt moments ago subsided. She gazed up at him and wondered how was it possible that each time they did this it was better than the time before. She always felt cherished in his arms.

Treasured.

Loved.

She silently shook that last thought away, refusing to let her mind go there; refusing to live on false hope. And she refused to give in to the want, need and desire to give him her heart again, no matter how strong the pull was to do so. She broke eye contact with him and looked away.

"Shelly?"

She returned her gaze to him, to respond to what he'd said. "It took a little longer than expected to get AJ settled tonight. He wanted us to have a long talk."

Dare asked, "Is he all right?"

"Yes. But I think he's somewhat disappointed that he didn't get the chance to tell you the truth today. He had planned to do so."

Dare sighed deeply. His gut instincts had been right. "Do you think I should talk to him tomorrow?"

Shelly shook her head. "No, I think the best thing to do is to wait until he gets up his courage again. But I suggest you make things a bit easier on him by making sure the two of you have absolute privacy without any interruptions. However, you're also going to have to make sure he doesn't think things are being orchestrated for that purpose. He still has to feel as though he's in control for a while longer,

Dare, especially with this. Right now, telling you that he's your son is very important to him."

Dare nodded. It was important to him as well. He slumped down on his back beside her and looked up at the stars. "I think I have an idea."

"What?"

"The brothers and I, along with Jamal, had planned on going to the cabin in the North Carolina mountains to go fishing. AJ knows about it since he heard us planning the trip, so he won't think anything about it. What if I invite him to come along?"

Shelly raised a brow. "Why would you want to take AJ with you guys? I'd think the six of you had planned it as a sort of guys' weekend, right?"

"Right. But I remember AJ mentioning to Thorn that he'd never gone fishing before, and I know that Thorn came close to inviting him. The only reason he didn't was because he knew we would he playing poker in addition to fishing and Storm's mouth can get rather filthy when he starts losing."

Shelly nodded. "But how will this help your situation with AJ? The two of you still won't have any privacy."

"Yes, we will if the others don't come. After AJ and I arrive, the others can come up with an excuse as to why they couldn't make it."

Shelly raised a doubtful brow. "All five of them?"

"Yes. It has to be a believable reason for all of them though, otherwise AJ will suspect something."

Shelly had to agree. "And while you and AJ are there alone for those three days, you think he'll open up to you?"

Dare sighed deeply. "I'm hoping that he will. At least I'm giving him the opportunity to do so." He met Shelly's stare. "What do you think?"

Shelly shrugged. "I don't know, Dare. It might be just

the thing, but I don't want you to get your hopes up and be disappointed. I know for a fact that AJ wants you to know the truth, but I also know that for him the timing has to be perfect."

Dare nodded as he pulled her into his arms. "Then I'm going to do everything in my power to make sure that it is."

Thirteen

Dare hung up the phone and met AJ's expectant gaze.

"That was Chase. One of his waitresses called in sick. He'll have to pitch in for the weekend and won't be able to make it."

He saw the disappointment cloud AJ's eyes. So far since arriving at the cabin they had received no-show calls from everyone except Thorn, and he expected Thorn to call any minute.

"Does that mean we have to cancel this weekend?" AJ asked in such a disappointed voice that a part of Dare felt like a heel. "Not unless you want to. There's still a possibility that Thorn might show."

Although he'd said the words, Dare knew they weren't true. His brothers and Jamal had understood his need to be alone with AJ this weekend and had agreed to bow out of the picture and plan something else to do.

When AJ didn't say anything, Dare said. "You know what I think we should do?"

AJ lifted a brow. "What?"

"Enjoy the three days anyway. I've been looking forward to a few days of rest and relaxation, and I'm sure you're glad to have an extra day out of school as well, right?"

AJ nodded. "Right."

"Then I say that we make the most of it. I can teach you how to fish in the morning and, tomorrow night we can camp outside. Have you ever gone camping?"

"No."

Dare sadly shook his head at the thought. When they were kids his father had occasionally taken him and his brothers camping for the weekend just to get them out of their mother's hair for a while. "We can still do all the things that we'd planned to do anyway. How's that?"

AJ was clearly surprised. "You'll want to stay here with just me?"

A lump formed in Dare's throat at the hope he heard in his son's voice. He swallowed deeply. *If only you knew how much I want to stay here with just you,* he thought. "Yes," he answered. "I guess I should be asking you if you're sure that you want to stay here with just me."

AJ smiled. "Yes, I want to stay."

Dare returned that smile. "Good. Then come on. Let's get the rest of the things out of the truck."

The next morning Dare got up bright and early and stood on the porch enjoying a cup of coffee. AJ was still asleep, which was fine, since the two of them had stayed up late the night before. Thorn had finally called to say he couldn't make it due to a deadline he had to meet for a bike he had to deliver. So it was final that it would only be the two of them.

After loading up the supplies in the kitchen after Thorn's

call, they'd gathered wood for a fire. Nights in the mountains meant wood for the fireplace and they had gathered enough to last all three days. Then, while he left AJ with the task of stacking the wood, Dare had gone into the kitchen to prepare chili and sandwiches for their dinner.

They hadn't said much over their meal, but AJ'd really started talking while they washed dishes. He'd told him about the friends he had left behind in California, and how he had written to them. They hadn't written back. He'd also talked about his grandparents, the Brockmans, and how he had planned to spend Christmas with them.

Now, Dare glanced around, deciding he really liked this place. It had once been jointly owned by one of their cousins and a friend of his, but Jamal had talked the two men into selling it to him and had then presented it to Delaney as one of her wedding gifts. It was at this cabin that Delaney and Jamal had met. While she was out of the country, Delaney had graciously given her brothers unlimited use of it, and all five had enjoyed getting away and spending time together here every once in a while.

Dare turned when he heard a noise behind him and smiled. "Good morning, AJ."

AJ wiped sleep from his eyes. "Good morning. You're up early."

Dare laughed. "This is the best time to catch fish."

AJ's eyes widened. "Then I'll be ready to go in a second." He rushed back into the house.

Dare chuckled and hoped his son remembered not only to get dressed but to wash his face and brush his teeth. He inhaled deeply, definitely taking a liking to this father business.

Dare smiled as he looked at the sink filled with fish. AJ had been an ace with the fishing pole and had caught just as many fish as he had. He began rolling up his sleeves to start cleaning them. They would enjoy some for dinner today and tomorrow and what was left they would take home with them and split between his mother and Shelly. Maybe he could talk Shelly into having a fish fry and inviting the family over.

His gaze softened as he thought how easy it was to want to include Shelly in his daily activities. He suppressed a groan thinking of all their nighttime activities and smiled as it occurred to him they had yet to make love in a bed. He had to think of a way to get her over to his place for the entire night. Sneaking off to make love in her backyard under the stars had started off being romantic, but now he wanted more than romance, he wanted permanence… forever. He wanted them to talk and plan their future, and he wanted her to know just how greatly she had enriched his life since she had returned.

He shifted his thoughts to AJ. So far they'd been together over twenty-four hours and he hadn't brought up the topic of their relationship. They had spent a quiet, leisurely day at the lake talking mostly about school and the Williams sisters. It seemed his son had a crush on the two tennis players in a big way, especially Serena Williams. Dare was glad he'd let Chase talk him into taking tennis lessons with him last summer; at least he knew a little something about the game and had been able to contribute to AJ's conversation.

Dare sighed, anxious to get things out in the open with AJ, but as Shelly had said, AJ would have to be the one to bring it up. He glanced over his shoulder when he heard his son enter the kitchen. He had been outside putting away their fishing gear.

"You did a good job today with that fishing rod, AJ," Dare said smiling over his shoulder. "I can't wait to tell Stone. The rod and reel you used belongs to him. He swears only a Westmoreland can have that kind of luck with it," he added absently.

"Then that explains things."

Dare turned around. "That explains what?"

"That explains why I did so good today—I *am* a Westmoreland."

Dare's breath caught and he swallowed deeply. He leaned back against the sink and stared at AJ long and hard, waiting for him to stop studying his sneakers and look at him. Moments later, AJ finally lifted his head and met his gaze.

"And how are you a Westmoreland, AJ?" Dare asked quietly, already knowing the answer but desperately wanting to hear his son say it anyway.

AJ cleared this throat. " I—I really don't know how to tell you this, but I have to tell you. And I have to first say that my mom wanted to tell you sooner, but I asked her not to, so it's not her fault so please don't be mad at her about it. You have to promise that you won't be mad at my mom."

Dare nodded. At that moment he would promise almost anything. "All right. I won't be mad at your mom. Now tell me what you meant about being a Westmoreland."

AJ put his hands into his pockets. "You may want to sit down for this."

Dare watched AJ's face and noticed how nervous he'd become. He didn't want to make him any more nervous than he already was, so he sat at the kitchen table. "Now tell me," he coaxed gently.

AJ hesitated, then met Dare's gaze, and said. "Although my last name is Brockman, I'm really a Westmore-land…because I'm your son."

Dare's breath got lodged in his throat. He blinked. Of course, the news AJ was delivering to him didn't surprise him, but the uncertainty and the caution he saw in his son's gaze did. Shelly had been right. AJ wasn't sure if he would accept him as his son, and Dare knew he had to tread lightly here.

"You're my son?" He asked quietly, as if for clarification.

"Yes. That's why I'm ten and that's why we have the same name." He looked down at his sneakers again as he added, "And that's why I look like you a little, although you haven't seem to notice but I'll understand if you don't want me."

Dare stood. He slowly crossed the room to AJ and placed what he hoped was a comforting hand, a reassuring hand, a loving hand on his shoulder. AJ looked up and met his gaze, and Dare knew he had to do everything within his power to make his son believe that he wanted him and that he loved him.

Choosing his words carefully and speaking straight from his heart and his soul, he said, "Whether you know it or not, you have just said words that have made me the happiest man in the entire world. The very thought that Shelly gave me a son fills me with such joy that it's overwhelming."

AJ searched his father's gaze. "Does that mean you want me?"

Dare chuckled, beside himself in happiness. "That means that not only do I want you, but I intend to keep you, and now that you're in my life I don't ever intend to let you out of it."

A huge smile crept over AJ's features. "Really?"

"Yes, really."

"And will my name get changed to Westmoreland?"

Dare smiled. "Do you want your name changed to Westmoreland?"

AJ nodded his head excitedly. "Yes, I'd like that."

"And I'd like that too. We'll discuss it with your mother and see what her feelings are on the matter, all right?"

"All right."

They stared at each other as the reality of what had taken place revolved around them. Then AJ asked quietly, "And may I call you Dad?"

Dare's chest tightened, his throat thickened and he became filled with emotions to overpowering capacity. He knew he would remember this moment for as long as he lived. What AJ was asking, and so soon, was more than he could ever have hoped for. He had prayed for this. A smile dusted across his face as parental pride and all the love he felt for the child standing in front of him poured forth.

"Yes, you can call me Dad," he said, as he reached out and pulled his son to him, needing the contact of father to son, parent to offspring, Westmoreland to Westmoreland. They shared a hug of acceptance, affirmation and acknowledgement as Dare fought back the tears in his eyes. "I'd be honored for you to call me that," he said in a strained voice.

Moments later, Dare sighed, thinking his mission should have been completed, but it wasn't. Now that he had his son, he realized more than ever just how much he wanted, loved and needed his son's mother. His mission wouldn't be accomplished until he had her permanently in his life as well.

Later that night Dare placed calls to his parents and siblings and told them the good news. They took turns talking with AJ, each welcoming him to the family. After dinner Dare and AJ had talked while they cleaned up the kitchen. Already plans were made for them to return to the cabin in a few months, and Dare suggested that they invite Shelly to come with them.

"She won't come," AJ said, drying the dish his father had handed him.

Dare raised a brow. "Why wouldn't she?"

"Because she's not going to be your girlfriend," he said softly. "Although now I wish that she would."

Dare turned and folded his arms across his chest and looked at his son. "And what makes you think your mother won't be my girlfriend, AJ?" he asked, although the title of wife was more in line with what he was aiming for.

"She told me," he said wryly. "That same night we had a cookout at Grandma and Grandpa Westmoreland's house. "After we got home we talked for a long time, and I told her that I had come close to telling you that night that I was your son. I asked if the three of us would be a family after I told you and she said no."

Dare remembered that night well. Shelly had been late coming to the backyard and had mentioned she and AJ had had a long talk. He sighed deeply as he tilted his head to the side to think about what AJ had said, then asked. "Did she happen to say why?"

AJ shook his head. "Yes. She said that although the two of you had been in love when you made me, that now you weren't in love anymore and were just friends. She also said that chances were that one day you would marry some-one nice and I'd have a second mother who would treat me like her son."

Dare frowned. He and Shelly not being in love was a crock. How could she fix her lips to say such a thing, let along think it? And what gave her the right to try and marry him off to some other woman? Didn't she know how he felt about her? That he loved her?

Then it suddenly hit him, right in the gut that, no, Shelly had no idea how he felt, because at no time had he told her. For the past month they had spent most of their time alone together, at night in her backyard under the stars making love. Did she think all they'd been doing was having sex?

But then why would she think otherwise? He sucked in a breath, thinking that he sure had missed the mark.

"Is that true, Dad? Will you marry someone else and give me a second mother?"

Dare shook his head. "No, son. Your mother is the only mother you'll have, and she's the only woman I ever plan to marry."

Mimicking his father, AJ placed his arms across his chest and leaned against the sink. "Well, I don't think she knows that."

Dare smiled. "Then I guess I'm just the person to convince her." He leaned closer to his son and with a conspiratorial tone, he said. "Listen up. I have a plan."

Fourteen

The first thing Shelly noticed as she entered the subdivision where Dare's home was located was that all the houses were stately and huge and sat on beautiful acreages. This was a newly developed section of town that had several shopping outlets and grocery stores. She could vividly remember it being a thickly wooded area when she had left town ten years ago.

She glanced at her watch. Dare had called and said that he and AJ had decided to return a day early and asked that she come over to his place and pick up AJ because Dare needed to stay at home and wait for the arrival of some important package. All of it sounded rather secretive, and the only thing she could come up with was that it pertained to some police business.

After reading the number posted on the front of the mailbox, she knew the regal-looking house that sat on a hill with a long, circular driveway belonged to Dare. She and Delaney had spent the day shopping yesterday and one of the things Delaney had mentioned was that Dare had banked most of his salary while working as a federal agent, and when he moved back home he had built a beautiful home.

Moments later, after parking her car Shelly strolled up the walkway and rang the doorbell. It didn't take long for Dare to answer.

"Hi, Shelly."

"Hi, Dare." Her heart began beating rapidly, thinking she would never tire of seeing him dressed casually in a pair of jeans and a chambray shirt. As she met his gaze, she thought that she had definitely missed him during the two days he and AJ had gone to North Carolina.

"Come on in," he invited, stepping aside.

"Thanks." She glanced around Dare's home when he closed the door behind her. Nice, she thought. The layout was open and she couldn't help noticing how chic and expensive everything looked. "Your home is beautiful, Dare."

"Thanks, and I'm glad you like it."

Shelly saw that he was leaning against the closed door staring at her. She cleared her throat. "You mentioned AJ finally got around to admitting that you're his father."

Dare shook his head. "Yes."

Shelly nodded. "I'm happy about that, Dare. I know how much you wanted that to happen."

"Yes, I did."

A long silence followed, and, with nothing else to say, Shelly cleared her throat again, suddenly feeling nervous in Dare's presence, mainly because he was still leaning against the door staring at her with those dark penetrating eyes of his. Breaking eye contact, she glanced at her watch and decided to end the silence. "Speaking of AJ, where is he?"

Dare didn't say anything for a moment, then he spoke. "He isn't here."

Shelly raised a brow. "Oh? Where is he?"

"Over at my parents. They dropped by and asked if he could visit with them for a while. I didn't think you would mind, so I told them he could."

Shelly nodded. "Of course I don't mind." After a few minutes she cleared her throat for the third time and said, "Well, I'm sure you have things to do so I'll—"

"No, I don't have anything to do, since the important package I was waiting for arrived already."

"Oh."

"In fact, I was hoping that you and I could take in a movie and have dinner later."

Her dark gaze sank into his. "Dinner? A movie?"

"Yes, and you don't have to worry about AJ. He'll be in good hands."

With a slight shrug, she said. "I know that, Dare. Your parents are the greatest."

Dare smiled. "Well, right now they think their oldest grandson is the greatest. Now that the secret is out, you should have seen my mom. She can't wait to go around bragging to everyone about him since it's safe to do so."

Shelly's stomach tightened. Now that the secret was out, things would be changing…especially her relationship with Dare. He wouldn't have to pretend interest in her any longer. Even now, she knew that probably the only reason he was inviting her to the movies and to dinner was out of kindness.

"Well, what about the movies and dinner?" Dare asked, reclaiming her attention.

She met his gaze. This would probably be the last time they would be together, at least out in public. There was no doubt in her mind that until they got their sexual needs under control they would still find the time to see each other at night in private.

"Yes, Dare. I'll go out to the movies and to dinner with you."

"Thanks for going out with me tonight, Shelly."

"Thanks for inviting me, Dare. I really enjoyed myself." And she had. They had seen a comedy featuring Eddie Murphy at the Magic Johnson Movie Theater near the Greenbriar Mall. Afterwards, they had gone to a restaurant that had served the best-tasting seafood she'd ever eaten. Now they were walking around the huge shopping mall that brought back memories of when they had dated all those years ago and had spent a lot of their time there on the weekends.

Dare claimed the reason he was in no hurry to end their evening was because he wanted to give his parents and siblings a chance to bond with AJ, and he thought the stroll through Greenbriar Mall would kill some time.

"How do you like the type of work you're doing now, working outside the hospital versus working inside?"

This was the first time he had ever asked her anything about her job since she'd moved back. "It took some getting used to, but I'm enjoying it. I get to meet a lot of nice people and because of the hours I work, I'm home with AJ more."

Dare nodded. "I never did tell you why I stopped being an agent for the Bureau, did I?"

Shelly shook her head. "No, you didn't."

Dare nodded again. He then told her all the things he had liked about working for the FBI and those things he had begun to dislike. Finally he told her the reason he had returned home.

"And do you like what you're doing now, Dare?" she couldn't help but ask him, since she of all people knew what a career with the FBI had meant to him.

"Yes, I like what I'm doing now. I feel I'm making more of a difference here than I was making with the Bureau. It's like I'm giving back to a community that gave so much to my brothers and me while we were growing up. It's a good feeling to live in a place where you have history."

Shelly had to agree. She enjoyed being back home and couldn't bear the thought of ever leaving again. Although she had lived in L.A. for ten years, deep down she had never considered it as her home.

She sighed and glanced down at her watch. "It's getting late. Don't you think it's time for us to pickup AJ? I don't want him to wear out his welcome with your folks."

Dare laughed, and the sound sent sensations up Shelly's body, making her shiver slightly. He thought she had shivered for a totally different reason and placed his arm around her shoulders, pulling her closer to him for warmth. "He'll never be able to wear out his welcome with my family, Shelly. Come on, let's go collect our son."

Three weeks later, Shelly sat outside alone on her porch swing as it slowly rocked back and forth. It was the third week in October and the night air was cool. She had put on a sweater, but the stars and the full moon were so beautiful she couldn't resist sitting and appreciating them both. Besides, she needed to think.

Ever since that night Dare had taken her to a movie and to dinner, he had come by every evening to spend time with AJ. But AJ wasn't the only person he made sure he spent time with. Over the past few weeks he had often asked her out, either to a movie, dinner or both. Then there was the time he had asked her to go with him to the wedding of one of his deputies.

She sighed deeply. Each time she had tried putting distance between them, he would succeed in erasing the distance. Then there were the flowers he continued to send each week. When she had asked him why he was still sending them, he had merely smiled and said because he enjoyed doing so. And she had to admit that she enjoyed receiving them. But still, she didn't want to put too much stock in Dare's actions and continued to see what he was doing as merely an act of kindness on his part. It was evident that he wanted them to get along and establish some sort of friendly relationship for AJ's sake.

The other thing that confused her was the fact that he no longer sought her out at night. Their late-night rendezvous in her backyard had abruptly come to an end the night Dare had taken her on their first date. He had offered her no explanation as to why he no longer came by late at night, and she had too much pride to ask him.

He came by each afternoon around dinnertime and she would invite him to stay, so she still saw him constantly. And at night, after AJ went to bed, he would sit outside on the porch swing with her and talk about how her day had gone, and she would ask him about his. Their talks had become a nightly routine, and she had to admit that she rather enjoyed them.

She shifted her thoughts to AJ. He was simply basking in the love that his father and the entire Westmoreland family were giving him. Dare had been right when he'd said all AJ had needed was to feel that he belonged. Each time she saw her son in one of his happy moods, she knew that he was glad as well as proud to be a part of the Westmoreland clan, and that she had made the right decision to return to College Park.

She stood, deciding to go inside and get ready for bed. Dare had left immediately after dinner saying he had to go to the station and finish up a report he was working on. As usual, before he left he had kissed her deeply, but otherwise he had kept his hands to himself. However, whenever he pulled her into his arms, she knew he wanted her. His erection was always a sure indicator of that fact. But she knew he was fighting his desire for her, which made things confusing, because she didn't understand why.

As she got ready for bed she continued to wonder what was going on with Dare. Why had he ended all sexual ties between them? Had he assumed she thought things were more serious between them than they really were because of their nightly meetings in her backyard?

As she closed her eyes she knew that if reality could not find her in his arms making love, that she would be there with him in the dreams she knew she would have that night.

Shelly smiled at Ms. Mamie. The older woman had broken her ankle two weeks ago and Shelly had been assigned as her home healthcare nurse. "I thought we had talked about you staying off your foot for a while, Ms. Mamie."

Ms. Mamie smiled. "I tried, but it isn't easy when I have so much to do."

Shelly shook her head. "Well, your ankle will heal a lot quicker if you follow my instructions," she said, rewrapping the woman's leg. She made it a point to check on Ms. Mamie at least twice a week, and she enjoyed her visits. Even with only one good leg, the older woman still managed to get around in her kitchen and always had fresh cookies baked when Shelly arrived.

"So, how are things going with you and the sheriff?"

Shelly looked up. "Excuse me?"

"You and the sheriff. How are the two of you doing? Everyone is talking about it."

Shelly frowned, not understanding. "They are talking about Dare and AJ or about me and Dare?"

"They are talking about you and Dare. Dare and AJ is old news. Everyone knew that boy was Dare's son even if

Dare was a little slow in coming around and realizing that fact Shelly's mind immediately took in what Ms. Mamie had said. She'd had no idea that she and Dare were now the focus of the towns peoples' attention. "Why are people talking about me and Dare?"

"Because everyone knows how hard he's trying to woo you."

Shelly stilled in her task and looked at Ms. Mamie. She couldn't help but grin at something so ridiculous. "Why would people think Dare is trying to woo me?"

"Because he is, dear."

The grin was immediately wiped from Shelly's face. Woo her? Dare? She shook her head. "I think you're mistaken."

"No, I'm not," Ms. Mamie answered matter-of-factly. "In fact, me and the ladies in my sewing club are taking bets."

Shelly raised a brow. "Bets?"

"Yes, bets as to whether or not you're going to give him a second chance. All of us know how much he hurt you before."

Shelly's head started spinning. "But I still don't understand why you all would think he was wooing me."

Ms. Mamie smiled. "Because it's obvious, Shelly. Luanne tells us each time he sends you flowers, which I understand is once, sometimes twice a week. Then, according to Clara, who lives across the street from you, he comes to dinner every evening and he takes you out on a date occasionally." The woman's smile widened. "Clara also mentioned that he's protecting your reputation by leaving your house at a reasonable time every night so he won't give the neighbors something to talk about."

Shelly shook her head. "But none of that means anything."

Ms. Mamie gently patted her hand. "That's where you're wrong, Shelly. It means everything, especially for a man like Dare. The ladies and I have watched him over the years ignore one woman after another, women who threw themselves at him. He never got serious about any of them. When you came back things were different. Anyone with eyes can see that he is smitten with you. That boy has always loved you, and I'll be the first to say he made a mistake ten years ago, but I feel good knowing he's trying real hard to win you back." She then grinned conspiratorially. "It even makes me feel good knowing that you're making it hard for him.

Making it hard for him? She hadn't even picked up on the fact that he was trying to win her back. Shelly opened her mouth to say something, then closed it, deciding that she needed to think about what Ms. Mamie had said. Was it true? Was Dare actually wooing her?

That question was still on her mind half an hour later when she pulled out of Ms. Mamie's driveway. She sighed deeply. The only person who could answer that question was Dare, and she decided it was time that he did.

Thunder rumbled in the distance as Dare placed a lid on the pot of chili he'd just made. He had tried keeping himself busy that afternoon since thoughts of Shelly weighed so heavily on his mind.

He knew one of the main reasons for this was that AJ would be spending the weekend with Morris and Cornelius, which meant Shelly would be home all alone, and Shelly all alone was too much of a temptation to think about. He sighed deeply, wondering just how much longer he could hold out in his plan to prove to her that what was between them was more than sex and that he cared deeply for her. For the past three weeks he had been the ardent suitor as he tried easing his way back into her heart. The only thing about it was that he wasn't sure whether his plan was working and exactly where he stood with her.

He paused in what he was doing when he heard his

doorbell ring and wondered which of his brothers had decided to pay him a visit. It would be just like them to show up in time for dinner. Leaving the kitchen, he made his way through the living room to open the front door. His chest tightened with emotion when he looked through his peephole and saw that it wasn't one of his brothers standing outside on his porch, but Shelly.

He quickly opened the door and recognized her nervousness. A man in his profession was trained to detect when someone was fidgety or uneasy about something. "Shelly," he greeted her, wondering what had brought her to his place.

"Dare," she said returning the greeting in what he considered a slightly skittish voice. "May I come in and talk to you about something?"

He nodded and said, "Sure thing," before stepping aside to let her enter.

His gaze skimmed over her as she passed him, and he thought there was no way a woman could look better than this, dressed in a something as simple as a pullover V-neck sweater and a long flowing skirt; especially if that skirt appeared to have been tailor-made just for her body. It flowed easily and fluidly down all her womanly curves.

He locked the door and turned to find her standing in the middle of his foyer as though she belonged in his house, every day and every night. "We can go into the living room if you like," he said trying not to let it show just how much he had missed being alone with her.

"All right."

He led her toward the living room and asked, "Are you hungry? I just finished making a pot of chili."

"No, thanks, I'm not hungry."

"What about thirsty? Would you like something to drink?"

.She smiled at him. "No, I don't want anything to drink. I'm fine."

He nodded. Yes, she was definitely fine. He didn't know another woman with a body quite like hers, and the memories of being inside that body made his hands feel damp. The room suddenly felt warmer than it should be.

He inhaled as he watched her take a seat on the sofa. He, in turn, took the chair across from her. Once she had gotten settled, he asked. "What is it you want to talk to me about, Shelly? Is something wrong with AJ?"

She shook her head. "Oh, no, everything with AJ is fine. I dropped him off at the Sears's house. I think he's excited about spending the weekend."

Dare nodded. He thought AJ was excited about spending the weekend as well. "If it's not about AJ then what do you want to talk about?"

His gaze held hers, and she hesitated only a moment before responding. "I paid a visit to Ms. Mamie today to check on her ankle. I'll be her home healthcare nurse for a while."

Dare nodded again, thinking there had to be more to her visit than to tell him that. "And?"

She hesitated again. "And she mentioned something that I found unbelievable, but I was concerned since it seems that a lot of the older women in this town think it's true."

He searched her features and detected more nervousness than before. "What do they think is true?"

Dare became concerned when seconds passed and Shelly didn't answer. Instead, she moved her gaze away from his to focus on some object on his coffee table. He frowned slightly. There had never been a time that Shelly had felt the need to be shy in his presence, so why was she now?

Standing, he crossed the room to sit next to her on the sofa. "All right, Shelly, what's this about? What do Ms. Mamie and her senior citizens' club think is true?"

Shelly swallowed deeply and took note of how close Dare was sitting next to her. Every time she took a breath she inhaled his hot male scent, a scent she had grown used to and one she would never tire of.

She breathed in and decided to come clean. Making light of the situation would probably make it easier, she thought, especially if he decided to laugh at something so absurd. She smiled slightly. "For some reason they think you're trying to woo me."

His gaze didn't flicker, but remained steadily on her face when he asked. "Woo you?"

She nodded. "Yes, you know—pursue me, court me."

Sitting so close to her, Dare could feel her tension. He also felt her uncertainty. "In other words," he said softly, "they think I'm trying to win you over, find favor in your eyes, in your heart and in your mind and break down your resistance."

Shelly nodded, although she didn't think Dare needed to break down her resistance since he had successfully done that a month or so ago. "Yes, that's it. That's what they believe. Isn't that silly?"

Dare shifted his position and draped his arms across the back of the sofa. He met Shelly's gaze, suddenly feeling hungry and greedy with an appetite that only she could appease. He studied her face for a little while longer, then calmly replied. "No, I don't think there's anything silly about it, Shelly. In fact, their assumptions are right on target."

She blinked once, twice, as the meaning of his words sank in. He watched as her eyebrows raised about as high as they could go, and then she said, "But why?"

Keeping his gaze fixed on hers, he asked. "Why what?"

"Why would you waste your time doing something like that?"

Dare drew in a deep breath. "Mainly because I don't

consider it a waste of my time, Shelly. Other than winning my son's love and respect, winning your heart back is the most important thing I've ever had to do."

Shelly swallowed, and for the first time in weeks she felt a bubble of hope grow inside her. Her heart began beating rapidly against her ribs. Was Dare saying what she thought he was saying? There was only one way to find out. "Tell me why, Dare."

He leaned farther back against the sofa and smiled. His smile was so sexy, so enticing, and so downright seductive that it almost took her breath away. "Because I wanted to prove to you that I knew the difference between having sex and making love. And I had the feeling that you were beginning to think I didn't know the difference, and that all those times we spent in your backyard on that blanket were about sex and had nothing to do with emotions. But emotions were what it was all about, Shelly, each and every time I took you into my arms those nights. I have never just had sex with you in my life. There has never been a time that I didn't make love to you. For us there will always be a difference."

Tears misted Shelly's eyes. He was so absolutely right. For them there would always be a difference. She had tried convincing herself that there wasn't a difference and that each time they made love it was about satisfying hormones and nothing more. But she'd only been fooling herself. She loved Dare. She had always loved him and would always love him.

"AJ made me realize what you might have been thinking when we spent time at the cabin together," Dare said, interrupting Shelly's thoughts.

"He told me what you had said about the possibility of me getting married one day, and I knew then what you must have been thinking to assume that you and AJ and I would never be a family."

Shelly nodded. "But we will be a family?" she asked quietly, wanting to reach out and touch Dare, just to make sure this entire episode was real and that she wasn't dreaming any of it.

"Yes, we will be a family, Shelly. I made a mistake ten years ago by letting you go, but I won't make the same mistake twice. I love you and I intend to spend the remainder of my days proving just how much." Sitting forward, his smile was tender and filled with warmth and love when he added. "That is, if you trust me enough to give me another chance."

Shelly reached out and cupped his jaw with her hands. She met the gaze of the man she had always loved and who would forever have her heart. "Are you sure that is what you want, Dare?"

"Yes, I haven't been more sure of anything in my life, Shelly, so make me the happiest man in the world. I love you. I always have and always will, and more than anything, I want you for my wife. Will you marry me?"

"Oh, Dare, I love you, too, and yes, I will marry you." She automatically went into his arms when he leaned forward and kissed her. His kiss started off gentle, but soon it began stoking a gnawing hunger that was seeping through both of their bodies and became hard and demanding. And then suddenly Dare broke the kiss as he stood and Shelly found herself lifted off the sofa and cradled close to his body.

While she slowly ran her lips along his jaw, the corners of his mouth and his neck, he took the stairs two at a time, his breath ragged, as he carried her to his bedroom. Once there, he placed her in the middle of his bed and began removing his shirt. Her mouth began watering as he exposed a hard-muscled chest. All the other times since she'd been back they had made love in the dark, and although she had felt his chest she hadn't actually seen it. At least not like this. It was daylight and she was seeing it all, the thatch of hair that covered his chest then tapered down into a thin line as it trailed lower to his...

She swallowed and realized that his hand had moved to the snap on his jeans. He slowly began taking them off. She swallowed again. Seeing him like this, in the light, a more mature and older Dare, made her see just how much his body had changed, just how much more physical, masculine and totally male he was.

And just how much she appreciated being the woman he wanted.

She watched as he reached into the nightstand next to the bed to retrieve a condom packet, and how he took the time to prepare himself to keep her safe. With that task done, he lifted his gaze and met hers. "I'd like other children, Shelly."

She smiled and said, "So would I, and I know for a fact that AJ doesn't like being an only child, so he would welcome a sister or brother as well."

Dare nodded, remembering the question AJ had asked about whether he wanted other children. He was glad to hear AJ would welcome the idea. Dare walked the few steps back over to the bed and, leaning down, he began removing every stitch of clothing from Shelly's body, almost unable to handle the rush of desire when he saw her exposed skin.

"You're beautiful, Shelly," he whispered breathless, smiling down at her when he had finished undressing her and she lay before him completely naked.

She returned his smile, glowing with his compliment. As he joined her in bed and took her into his arms, she knew that this was where she had always been meant to be.

Shelly felt the heat of desire warm her throat the moment Dare joined his mouth to hers, and all the love she had for him seeped through every part of her body as his kiss issued a promise she knew he would fulfill.

They hadn't made love in over a month so she wasn't surprised or shocked by the powerful emotions surging through her that only intensified with Dare's kiss. He wasn't just kissing her, he was using his tongue to stroke a need, deliver a promise and strip away any doubt that it was meant for them to be together.

Dare dragged his mouth from hers, his breath hard, shaky and harsh. "I need you now, baby," he said, reaching down and checking her readiness and finding her hot and wet. He settled his body over hers as fire licked through his veins, love flowed from his heart and a need to be joined with her drove everything within him.

He inhaled sharply as the tip of his erection pressed her wet and swollen flesh and it seemed that every part of his being was focussed there, and when she opened legs wider for him, arched her back, pushed her hips up and sank her nails deep in his shoulder blades, he couldn't help but groan and surge forward. The sensation of him filling her to the hilt only made him that much more hungrier, greedy. And she was there with him all the way.

He thrust into her again and again, each stroke more hard and determined than the one before; the need to mate life staining, elemental, a necessity. And when he felt her thighs begin to quiver with the impact of her release, he followed her, right over the edge into oblivion. This woman who had given him a little Dare, who gave him more love than he rightly deserved would have his heart forever.

A shiver of awareness course down the length of Shelly's spine when Dare placed several kisses there. She opened her eyes and met his warm gaze.

"Do you know this is the first time we've made love in a bed since you've been back," he said huskily, as an amused smile touched his lips.

She tipped her head to the side and smiled. "Is that good or bad?"

His long fingers reached out and begin skimming a path from her waist toward the center of her legs. "It's better." He leaned down and placed a kiss on her lips. "Stay with me tonight."

The heat shimmering in his eyes made her body fever-ish. With AJ spending the weekend away there was no problem with her staying with him. "Umm, what do I get if I stay?" She closed her eyes and sighed when his fingers touched her, caressed her, intent on a mission to drive her insane.

"Do you have to ask?" he rasped, his voice low and teas-ing against her lips.

"No, I don't," she replied in breathless anticipation.

She trembled as Dare began inflaming her body the same way he had inflamed her heart. They had endured a lot, but through it all their love had survived and for the first time since returning to College Park, she felt she had finally come home.

Epilogue

A month later

Shelly couldn't help but notice the frown on the Dare's face. It was a frown directed at Storm, who had just kissed her on the lips.

"I thought I warned you about doing that, Storm," Dare said in a very irritated tone of voice.

"But I can get away with it today because she's the bride and any well-wisher can kiss a bride on her wedding day."

Dare raised a brow. "Are you also willing to kiss the groom?"

Now it was Storm who frowned. "Kiss you? Hell no!"

Dare smiled. "Then I suggest you keep your lips off the bride," he said, bringing Shelly closer to his side. "And there's enough single women here for you to kiss so go try your lips on someone else."

Storm chuckled. "The only other woman I'd want to kiss is Tara and I'm not crazy enough to try it. You're all talk, but Thorn really *would* kill me."

Shelly chuckled at Storm's comment as her gaze went to the woman the brothers had labeled Thorn's challenge, Tara Matthews. She was standing across the room talking to Delaney. Shelly thought that Tara was strikingly beautiful in an awe-inspiring, simply breathtaking way, and she couldn't help noticing that most of the men at the reception, both young and old, were finding it hard to keep their eyes off her. Every man except for Thorn. He was merely standing alone on the other side of the room looking bored.

"How can the two of you think that Thorn is interested in Tara when he hasn't said anything to her at all, other than giving her a courtesy nod? And he's not paying her any attention."

Dare chuckled. "Oh, don't let that nonchalant look fool you. He's paying her plenty of attention, right down to her painted toenails. He's just doing a good job of pretending not to."

"Yeah," Storm chimed in, grinning. "And he's been brooding ever since Delaney mentioned at breakfast this morning that Tara is moving to Atlanta to finish up her residency at a hospital here. The fact that she'll be in such close proximity has Thorn sweating. The heat is on and he doesn't like it at all."

A short while later Dare and Shelly had a talk with their son. "It's almost time for us to leave for our cruise, AJ. We want you on your best behavior with Grandma and Grandpa Westmoreland."

"All right." AJ looked at his father with bright eyes. "Dad, Uncle Chase and Uncle Storm said all of us are going fishing when you get back."

Dare smiled. He had news for his brothers. If they thought for one minute that he would prefer spending a weekend with them rather than somewhere in bed with his wife, they had another thought coming. "Oh, they did, did they?"

"Yes."

He nodded as he glanced over at his brothers who were talking to Tara—all of them except for Thorn. He also noted the Westmoreland cousins—brothers Jared, Durango, Spencer, Ian and Reggie—were standing in the group as well. The only one missing was Quade, and because of his covert activities for the government, there was no telling where that particular Westmoreland was or what he was doing at any given moment. "We'll talk about it when I get back," Dare said absently to AJ, wondering at the same time just where Thorn had gone off to. Although he didn't see him, he would bet any amount of money that he was somewhere close by with his eyes on Tara.

Dare shrugged. He was glad Tara was Thorn's challenge and not his. He then returned his full attention to his son. "When school is out for the holidays, your mom and I are thinking about taking you to Disney World."

"Wow!"

Dare chuckled. "I take it you'd like that?"

"Yes, I'd love it. I've been to Disneyland before but not Disney World and I've been wanting to go there."

"Good." Dare pulled Shelly into his arms after checking his watch. It was time for them to leave for the airport. They would be flying to Miami to board the cruise ship to St. Thomas. "And keep an eye on your uncles, AJ, while I'm gone. They have a tendency to get a little rowdy when I'm not here to keep them in line."

AJ laughed. "Sure, Dad."

Dare clutched AJ's shoulder and pulled him closer. "Thanks. I knew that I could count on you."

He breathed in deeply as he gathered his family close. With Shelly on one side and AJ on the other, he felt intensely happy on this day, his wedding day, and hoped that each of his brothers and cousins would one day find this same happiness. It was well worth all the time and effort he had put into it.

When he met Shelly's gaze one side of his mouth tilted into a hopelessly I-love-you-so much smile, and the one she returned said likewise. And Dare knew in his heart that he was very happy man.

His mission had been accomplished. He had won the hearts of his son and of the woman that he loved.

* * * * *

Please turn the page
for an exciting preview of

LUCKY
by
Jennifer Greene

Coming in July 2005 from
Harlequin Next!

Prologue

DAMNED IF HER HANDS weren't shaking.

Kasey sighed in exasperation. A year ago, she could never have imagined this moment—but then, a year ago, she'd believed she was the luckiest woman alive.

Thunder grumbled in the west as she hurried into the baby's dark bedroom. Tess was lying in her crib, gnawing on a teething ring, wearing nothing but a diaper. Michigan in August was often hot, but this intense, smothering heat just kept coming. Normally Tess would have long been asleep by now, but the looming storm must have wakened her.

Curtains billowed wildly in the hot, nervous wind. Clouds hurtled across the sky, bringing pitchforks of sterling-silver lightning and a hiss of ozone. When the first fat raindrops smacked against the windows, lights flickered on and off—not that Kasey cared. She wasn't worried whether the house lost power. She was worried whether she might.

She was born gutless. Pulling enough courage together

to leave tonight was taking everything she had, everything she was—and she was still afraid that might not be enough.

"But you're up for a little adventure, aren't you, love bug?"

The baby kicked joyfully at the sound of her mother's voice.

"That's it. We're just going to be calm and quiet, okay?" Well, one of them was. The baby softly babbled as Kasey swiftly changed her diaper and threaded on a lightweight sleeper.

A short time before, she'd stashed suitcases in the back of the Volvo, but she couldn't leave quite yet. Quickly she packed a last bag with critical items—not diapers or clothes or money—but the things that mattered, like the jewel-colored mobile, the handmade quilt, and of course, the red velvet ball.

She juggled Tess and the bag, taking the back stairs, her heart slamming so hard she could hardly think. She grabbed rain gear on the way out. The garage was darker than a dungeon, yet Tess—who should have been tired enough to pull off a good, cranky tantrum—settled contentedly in her car seat. Kasey tossed in the rest of their debris and plunked down in the front.

It bit, taking the six-year-old Volvo. It wasn't a car she'd paid for. It wasn't a car she'd chosen. But compared to the new Mercedes and the sleek black Lotus and the Lexus SUV, it was the cheapest vehicle in the fleet, and God knew, the Volvo was built like a tanker.

A sturdy car wasn't going to do her much good if she couldn't get it moving, yet initially her fingers refused to cooperate. Yanking and snapping on the seat belt seemed to present an epic challenge. Then the key refused to fit in the lock. Finally she started the engine—which sounded like a sonic boom to her frantic ears—and then she almost forgot to push the garage door opener before backing out.

Her gaze kept shooting to the back door. Waiting for it to open. Afraid it would open. No matter how well she'd planned, no matter what she'd said, she was still afraid something or someone would find a way to stop her from leaving, stop her from taking Tess.

In an ideal world, she'd have made contingency plans—but she hadn't been living in an ideal world for a long time now. She had no alternate plans, no contingency ideas.

This was it. Her one shot to tear apart her entire life in one fell swoop.

That thought was so monumentally intimidating that she considered having a full-scale nervous breakdown—but darn it, she didn't have time. Her hand coiled on the gear-shift and jerked it in Reverse. The instant the car cleared the driveway, she gunned the accelerator.

Rain slooshed down in torrents, blurring her vision of the house and neighborhood. For so long she'd thought of Grosse Pointe as her personal Camelot. It struck her with a flash of irony that it really had been. She was the one who'd goofed up the happy-ever-after ending. She'd not only failed to follow the fairy-tale script, she'd somehow turned into the wicked character in the story.

Kasey knew people believed that. For months, she'd believed herself at fault, too—but no more.

She leaned forward, fooling with knobs and buttons. The windshield wipers struggled valiantly to keep up with the rain, but the defroster was losing ground. Steam framed the edges of the windows, creating a surreal, smoky world where it seemed as if nothing existed but her and the baby.

Kasey spared a quick, protective glance at her daughter. In that tiny millisecond, her heart swelled damn near to burst-ing. She'd never imagined the fierce, warm, irrevocable bond between mother and child until she'd had Tess. Sometimes she thought that love was bigger than both of them.

It still struck her as amazing, what even a spineless wuss—such as herself—would do for her child. And for love.

Emotions clogged in her throat, welled there, jammed there. Even now, she knew she could turn back. It was hard, not to want to be safe. Hard, to believe she had what it took to take this road.

By the standards of another life—the life she'd been living a year ago—Kasey knew absolutely that others would judge her behavior as wrong. Dead wrong, morally and ethically wrong, wrong in every way a woman could define the word.

A sudden clap of thunder shook the sky. The storm was getting worse, lightning scissoring and slashing the sky over the lake. When Kasey turned onto Lakeshore Drive, Lake St. Clair was to her left, the water black and wild and spitting foam. There were no boats on the lake, no cars on the road. No one else was anywhere in sight.

Sane people had the sense to stay home in storms this rough.

At the first traffic light, she whipped her head around again, but Tess didn't need checking on. The baby was wide awake and staring intently at the car windows, where streetlights reflected in the rain drooling down the glass.

The look in the baby's eyes warmed Kasey. It didn't suddenly miraculously make their situation all right—nothing could do that. But it was so easy to think of the storm as uncomfortable and unpleasant. Through the baby, Kasey saw the night diamonds, the magic in rain and light. Her vulnerable daughter had bought her miracles in every sense of the word.

Whatever frightening or traumatic things happened from here, she was simply going to have to find a way to cope with them.

The instant the traffic light turned green, she zoomed

through the intersection. Quickly the lake disappeared behind them. The long sweeps of velvet lawns and elegant estates turned into ordinary streets. Lakeshore Drive changed its name when it got past the ritzy stuff. Kasey started sucking in great heaps of air at the same time.

The extra oxygen didn't particularly help. She still couldn't make her pulse stop zooming, her hands stop shaking. But it was odd. She didn't really mind being shook up to beat the band. At least those feelings were real. She didn't have to hide being anxious, being afraid—being who she was—anymore.

Love had the power to change a woman.

Kasey would never doubt that again.

The trick, of course, was for a woman to be able to tell the difference between life-transforming love and the kind of love that could destroy her.

She ran a yellow light. Then another. Courage started coming back in slow seeps. Of course, she was nervous and afraid. Who wouldn't be?

She knew where she was going now. It was just hard to stop the questions from spinning in her mind.

How could she possibly have come to this point?

How did a nice, quiet, decent woman who'd always played by the rules get herself into such a situation?

How had the dream of her life become such a soul-destroying nightmare?

But the answers, of course, couldn't be found in this night. The answers were steeped in the events over the past year. In fact, the whole story began almost a year ago to the day....

1

"FOR GOD'S SAKE, KASEY. No one's killing you. You're just having a baby!"

"Yeah, well, they told me all the pain would be in my head. None of it's in my head!"

"Yelling and swearing isn't going to help."

Well, actually, she thought it might. She should have known it would happen to her this way. Breaking her water at a party—right in front of people she wanted to respect her, people Graham respected. Still, knowing she was going to die within the next hour definitely helped. It was a little depressing, realizing that people's last memory of her would be with bloody water gushing down her legs in the middle of a dinner party. On the other hand, she'd be dead, so what was the point in worrying about it? For the same reason, there didn't seem much point not to howl her heart out when the next pain hit, either.

As far as she could tell, she wasn't likely to live through the next pain anyway.

"You wanted this baby," Graham reminded her.

"Oh, Graham, I do. I do."

"So try and get a grip. We'll be at the hospital in fifteen minutes. Just stay here. I'll run upstairs and get your suitcase and some towels for the car…."

He was gone, leaving Kasey in the kitchen alone for those few minutes. She sank against the white tile counter as another contraction started to swell.

Something was wrong with her. It wasn't the stupid pain. They'd all lied about the pain—and she was going to stay alive long enough to kill the Lamaze instructor who promised that labor was simply work. It wasn't work. It was torture, cut and dried. Yet Kasey fiercely, desperately, wanted this baby, and had expected to feel joyous when the blasted labor process finally started.

Instead, she felt increasingly overcome by a strange, surreal sense of panic. Goofy thoughts kept pouncing in her mind. This wasn't her house. This wasn't her life. This wasn't really happening to her.

As the contraction finally ebbed, leaving her forehead flushed with sweat, she stared blankly around the high-tech kitchen. She realized perfectly well that anxiety was causing those foolish thoughts, yet the acres of stainless steel appliances and miles of white tile really *didn't* seem to be hers. She'd never have chosen a white floor for a kitchen. The doorway led to a dining room with ornate Grecian furniture that she'd never chosen, either. The dining room led into a great room with cream carpeting and cream furniture—Graham had chosen all that stuff before they'd married, wanting a neutral color like crème to set off the artwork on the walls. He was a collector.

But now, the more she looked around, the more she felt

a building panic roaring in her ears. This whole last year, she'd basked in a feeling of BEING LUCKY so big, so rich, so magical that she just wanted to burst with it. She'd found a true prince in Graham, when at thirty-eight, she'd given up believing she'd find anyone at all. And living in Grosse Pointe was like living in her own private Camelot—which it was, it really was. It was just that this crazy panic was blindsiding her. Maybe it had all been a dream. She didn't live here. How could she possibly live here? She didn't DO elegant. Cripes, she didn't even LIKE elegant.

Not that she'd ever complained. Graham had said too many times that his ex-wife, Janelle, had been a nonstop complainer.

It wasn't as if she spent much time in the fancy-dancy parts of the house, besides. With the baby coming, the kitchen was the room that mattered, and all the high-tech appliances were a cook's dream. Still, the dishes were bone china. Heirlooms. Beautiful—but it was darn hard to imagine a baby in a high chair, drinking milk from a lead crystal glass and slopping up cereal from a 22-karat-gold rimmed bowl onto that virgin-white tile floor.

Shut up, Kasey. Just shut your mind up. Another pain was coming. This one felt like lightning on the inside, as if something sharp and jagged was trying to rip her apart. Then came the twisting sensation, as if an elephant were swollen in her stomach and trying to squeeze through a space smaller than a spy hole.

She opened her mouth to scream her entire heart out, when Graham suddenly jogged into the room. "All right, I reached Dr. Armstrong. He'll meet us at the hospital. You holding up okay?"

Of course she wasn't okay. She couldn't conceivably be less okay. She was wrinkled, stained, shaky, and positively within minutes of death by agony. Graham, typically, looked ready to host a yacht-club outing. Abruptly—and with all the grace of a walrus—she pushed away from the counter and aimed for the back door. "Which car are we taking?"

"The Beemer. Easiest to clean the leather seats if we have to. Although I brought towels."

For an instant she thought, *Come on, Graham, couldn't you think for one second about the baby instead of fussing over getting a stain in a car?* But even letting that thought surface shamed her.

Her attitude had sucked all day, when she knew perfectly well that Graham was unhappy about the coming baby. During their courtship, he'd been bluntly honest about wanting no children—he adored his nearly grown daughter, but that was the point. He'd done the fatherhood thing. At this life stretch he wanted Kasey, alone, a romantic relationship with just the two of them.

Maybe there was a time when Kasey fiercely wanted children, but even at thirty-eight, there were increased health risks with a pregnancy. More than that, she'd already settled into a life without kids—and she loved Graham and everything about her life with him, so it just wasn't that hard to go along with his choice.

Birth control hadn't failed them so much as life had. She'd tracked conception down to the week she'd had a bad flu and couldn't hold anything down—including her birth control pills. By the time she'd recovered, the fetus already had a grab-hold on life. If the problem had never happened, Kasey would undoubtedly have been happy as things were—but once she realized that she was pregnant...well, there was only one chance of a baby for her. This one.

She wanted this baby more than she wanted her own breath, even her own life. It was her one shot at motherhood. She just couldn't give it up.

And she totally understood that Graham wasn't happy about it—but there was no fixing that yet. Once the baby was born, she could work on him, make sure he never felt neglected, take care to shower him with love. Besides which, once the baby was born and Graham held the little one, Kasey felt certain the baby would win his heart. It'd all work out.

If she just didn't blow it in the meantime.

"I love you," she said in the car.

"I love you, too, hon." But immediately he fell silent, steering through the quiet night, his profile pale as chalk. Dribbles accumulated on the windshield. Not rain, just the promise of it. She heard a siren somewhere, the thunk of the occasional windshield wiper, and realized that she was doing better. The pains were easing up, not one galloping right after the other now.

Randolph Hospital loomed ahead. Graham pulled up to the Emergency Room door where a sign read No Parking Under Any Circumstances. The hospital looked more like an elegant estate than a medical facility, with security lights glowing on the landscaped grounds and garden sculptures.

Graham slammed out of the car. "I'll get a wheelchair or a gurney. I hate to leave you alone, Kasey, but I promise I'll be right back."

"I'll be fine."

But she wasn't fine. He'd barely disappeared inside before another lumpy gush of blood squeezed between her legs. How come no one ever said labor was a total-gross out? Certainly not that nauseatingly cheerful Lamaze instructor. And then another pain sliced her in half, so sharp, so mean, that she couldn't catch her breath.

Pain was one thing. Being scared out of her mind was another. She fumbled for the door handle, thinking that she'd crawl inside the hospital if she had to—anything was better dying here alone in the dark. She got the door open. Got both feet out. But then the cramping contraction took hold and owned her. She cried out—to hell with bravery and pride and adulthood and how much she wanted this baby. If she lived through this, and that was a big *IF*, she was never having sex again, and that was for damn sure.

The emergency room doors swung open. She didn't actually notice the man until she heard the clip of boot steps jogging toward her, and suddenly he was there, hunkering down by the open curb.

"You need help?"

"No, no. Yes. I mean—my husband's coming. It's just that right now—" The pain was just like teeth that bit and ripped.

"What do you want me to do? Get you inside? Stay with you? What? I can carry you—"

"No. It' s—no. Just stay. Please. I—" She wasn't really looking at him, wasn't really seeing him. Her whole world right then was about babies and labor and pain. Still, there was something about him that arrested her attention. Something in his face, his eyes.

Their whole conversation couldn't have taken two minutes. She only really saw him in a flash. Background light dusted his profile, sharpened his features. He was built tall and lanky, with dark eyes and hair, had to be in his early forties or so. His clothes were nondescript, the guy-uniform in Grosse Pointe of khakis and polo shirt, but his looked more worn-in than most. *He* looked more worn-in than most. The thick, dark hair was walnut, mixed with a little cinnamon. The square chin had a cocky tilt, the shoulders an attitude—but it was his eyes that hooked her.

He had old eyes. Beautiful brown eyes. Eyes that held a lot of pain, had seen a lot of life. In the middle of the private hospital parking lot, mosquitoes pesking around her neck, panting out of the contraction, scared and hot...yet she felt a pull toward him. He exuded some kind of separateness, a loneliness.

She knew about loneliness.

Of course, that perception took all of a minisecond—and suddenly the emergency room doors were clanging open again. The man glanced up, then back at her. "Damn. You're Graham Crandall's wife? And you're having your baby in *this* hospital?"

His question and tone confused her. She started to answer, but there was never a chance. Graham noticed the man, said something to him—called him "Jake"—but then he disappeared from her sight. The world descended on her. In typical take-charge fashion, Graham had brought out an entire entourage—a wheelchair, three people in different medical uniforms, Dr. Armstrong.

Graham was midstream in conversation to the doctor. "I don't care what you have to do. She comes first. No exceptions, no discussion. You make sure she's all right and gets through this. And I want her to have something for the pain. Immediately."

"Mr. Crandall—Graham—first, I need to examine her, and then everything else will follow in due course. I swear that I've never yet lost a father—"

"I don't want to hear your goddamn reassuring patter, and forget trying to humor me. I want your promise that nothing is going to happen to my wife."

"Graham." Kasey had to swallow. She'd never seen her husband out of control. Graham didn't *do* out of control. And love suddenly swelled through her, putting the pain in perspective, reassuring her like nothing else could have. "I'm just having a baby. Really, I'm fine. The pain scared me. I didn't realize it was going to be this bad—"

"I'll take care of this, Kasey." Graham cut her off, and

rounded on Dr. Armstrong again. "I don't care what it costs. I don't care how many people or what it takes—you don't let anything happen to my wife. You understand?"

The next few hours were a blur of hospital lights and hospital smells. The labor room was decorated to look like a living room, with a chintz couch and TV and even a small kitchenette. Dr. Armstrong did the initial exam. As always, he was patient and calm and as steadfast as a brick.

"But I can't be only three centimeters dilated! You have to be kidding! I thought I was in transition because of the amount of pain."

"I'm going to give you something to help you relax, Kasey."

"I don't want to relax! I want to get to ten centimeters and get this over with! And I want to be able to see the fetal monitor! Is our baby okay?"

"Your baby's just fine," Dr. Armstrong said reassuringly, but he hadn't even looked. What was the point of being all trussed up with the fetal monitor if no one was even going to look at it? "You can have ice chips. And your husband can rub your back. And you can watch TV or listen to music…."

She just wanted it over with. But at least, once they all left her alone with Graham, she thought she could get a better hold on her fears and emotions. Later—an hour, or two, who knew?—she remembered the man outside, and thought to ask Graham who he was.

"Name is Jake McGraw. Used to be from the neighborhood."

"I thought you called him by name, so I was pretty sure you knew him."

"Yeah, I knew him. He's Joe's son. You've heard of Joe, used to be one of GM's high-step attorneys. Money from generations back. Joe had a heart attack a while ago, put

Jake back in the neighborhood now and then to help his father."

"So that's why he was at the hospital?" God. Another pain was coming on. How many did you get before you'd paid your dues? And now she knew you didn't die from the little ones, because there were lots, lots, *lots* bigger ones after that.

"I don't know why he was at the hospital. Forget him, Kasey. He's a loser. An alcoholic."

"Really?" For an instant she pictured those old, beautiful eyes again.

"Was part of a big fancy law firm, wife from the Pointe, fast lane all the way. Had a wild marriage, and I mean capital *W* wild. Gave one party that started out in GP and ended up in Palm Springs. They both played around, until some point when Jake went off the deep end. Or so they say. He's got a teenage son, Danny, lives with his ex-wife. Doesn't practice law anymore. You hearing me? He's bad news all the way. Lost everything. And deserved to."

"You never mentioned him before—"

"Why would I? And it beats me why we're talking about him now."

And then they weren't. She'd only asked the question in passing. The man wasn't on her mind. Nothing was, as the minutes wore on and the night deepened and darkened. Somewhere in the wing, a woman screamed. A door was immediately closed, sealing out the sound. The nurse came and went. Graham survived for a while—at least the first couple hours—but then he started pacing.

"Do you want some more ice chips, Kase? Are you cold? Warm? Want to watch any specific show on the tube?"

His solicitousness was endearing—except that every time a pain ripped through her, he paced again, like a panther who wanted to throw himself against the bars. Anything—but be trapped in here. "Graham, go out," she said finally.

"No way. I'm not leaving you."

"I know you're willing to stay. But this is hard...harder than I thought. And to be honest, I believe I'll handle the pain better if I'm alone. I've always been that way. Go on, you. Go get some coffee, or something to eat. Don't feel guilty, just go."

He kissed her, hard, on the forehead, squeezed her hand. But eventually she talked him into leaving.

She'd lied about wanting to be alone. The truth was, she desperately wanted Graham to be with her, yet he was obviously miserable, seeing her in pain. And for a while, for a long time, the fear completely left. Medical help was just a call away, and so was her husband, so it seemed easier to relax. She inhaled the silence. The peace. The feeling as if there was no one in the universe but her and the baby.

She cut all the lights but one, shut off the television. In between contractions, she rubbed her tummy, talking softly to her baby. This was about the two of them. No one else. "You're going to love your room. I bought you a teddy bear the size of a Santa, and the toy box is already filled. The wallpaper is balloons in jewel colors, and over your crib, I set up real jewels dangling from a mobile—amethyst, citrine, jade, pink quartz. When the sun comes, you won't believe what brilliant crystal patterns it makes on the wall. And there's a wonderful, big old rocker. You and I are going to rock and sing songs, and I'm never going to let you cry, never...."

An hour passed, then another. Suddenly a pain seared through her that was different from all the others.

Finally, she thought, the transition stage. All the books claimed this stage was the hardest—but it also meant that they were nearing the end. Soon enough she'd hold the real baby in her arms after all these months.

Another pain. Just like that one, only worse. More of the fire, more of the scalding feeling of being ripped apart. She hit the button for the nurse, then hit it again.

No one came.

Now she realized what a sissy she'd been before, because these contractions were completely different. And possibly that's why no one was coming now, because they thought she'd been crying wolf? Only Graham…where was he? Surely they wouldn't leave her much longer without someone checking on her?

This wasn't pain where she could scream or yell like before. This was pain so intense that it took all her concentration to just endure. This wasn't about whining how she could die; this was about believing for real that she may not survive this. Agony lanced through her, again and again, not ceasing, not letting up, not giving her a chance to catch her breath. Her body washed in sweat. Fear filled her mind like clouds in a stormy sky, pushing together, growling and thundering. She wanted her mom. She wanted Graham. She wanted someone, anyone. She pushed and pushed and pushed the call button, but she had no possible way to get up out of bed and seek help on her own, not by then.

Finally the door opened a crack. Then a nurse's voice. "Good God." Then…lights and bodies and motion and more pain. "There, Kasey, you're doing good—it's going to be all over very soon." By then she didn't care any more—or, if she cared, she couldn't find the energy to respond.

They wheeled her into an unfamiliar room. Stuck her with needles. "Where's Graham?" she asked, but no one answered. Everyone was running, running. The baby seemed to be rushing, rushing. And the pain was there, but with that last hypodermic, the knife edges of pain blunted, and her mind started blurring.

Somewhere, though, she heard a woman's voice. One of the nurse's. Low, urgent. "Doctor, there's something—"

She tried to stir through the thick mental fuzz, recognizing that something was happening. Something alarming. She heard the doctor's sharp, "Be quiet." And then, "Get out of the way. Let me see."

"Is something wrong?" she whispered.

No one answered.

"Doctor, is something wrong with my baby?"

Still no one answered. But she felt another needle jab in her arm. And immediately came darkness.

HER DREAMS WERE ALL SWEET, dark, peaceful. She remembered nothing until she heard the sound of a nurse's cheerful voice, and opened her eyes to a room full of sunshine. "Are we awake, Mrs. Crandall? I'm bringing your beautiful daughter. There you go, honey…I have on your chart that you want to nurse, so I'm going to help you get set up. Can we sit up?"

She pushed herself to a sitting position, listening to the nurse, taking in the pale blue walls of the private room, the fresh sun pouring in the window, the washed-clean sky of a new day. All those sensory perceptions, though, came from a distance.

Once the bundle was placed in her arms, there was only her and her daughter.

OhGodOhGodOhGod. The pain and fear had all been real, but mattered no more now than spit in a wind.

The feel of her daughter was magic. Reverently she touched the pink cheek, the kiss-me-shaped little mouth, then slowly—so carefully!—unwrapped the blanket. She counted ten fingers, ten toes, one nose, no teeth. Without question, her daughter was the first truly perfect thing in the entire world. Love rolled over Kasey in waves, fierce, hot, compelling, bigger than any avalanche and tidal wave put together.

"She's all right? *Really* all right? I remember the doctor sounding worried in the delivery room. I was scared something was going wrong—"

The nurse glanced at the chart at the bottom of the bed, then quickly turned away. "She sure looks like a healthy little princess to me." Efficiently the nurse adjusted Kasey's nightgown, and finally coaxed Kasey to quit examining the baby long enough to see mom and daughter hooked up. "I'm going to give you two a few private minutes, but I'll check on you in a bit, okay?"

Kasey nodded vaguely. The nurse was nice—but not part of her world. Not then. She stroked and cuddled her miracle as the little one learned to nurse.

She and Graham had bickered about baby names for months. Boys' names had been tough enough, but girls had seemed impossible. Cut and dried, Graham wanted Therese Elizabeth Judith if the child was a girl. Kasey thought that sounded like a garbled mouthful…now, though, she found a solution to the problem in an instant. Graham could have whatever name he wanted on the birth certificate.

But her name was Tess.

Kasey knew. From the first touch, the first smell and texture and look…the name simply fit her. And it was hard to stop cherishing and marveling. The little one had blue eyes—unseeing but beautiful. Her skin had the translucence of pearl. The head was pretty darn bald, but there was a hint of rusty-blond fuzz. Little. Oh, she was so little.

Kasey thought, *I'd do anything for you.* And was amazed at the compelling swamp of instincts. How come no one had told her how fierce the emotion was? That mom-love was this powerful, this extraordinarily huge?

"Oh, Graham," she murmured as she caressed the little one's head. "Wait until you see how precious, how priceless your daughter is. She's worth anything. Everything. All…"

Kasey stopped talking on a sudden swallow. She looked up.

Darn it—where *was* Graham?

JAKE PULLED HIS eight-year-old Honda Civic into the driveway on Holiday, touched the horn to announce his arrival, and then walked around and climbed into the passenger seat.

He saw the living room curtain stir, so Danny heard the car—but that was no guarantee his son would emerge from the house in the next future. Rolling down the window—it was hot enough to fry sweat—he reached in the back seat for his battered briefcase. Sweet, summery flowers scented the late afternoon, but the humidity was so thick it was near choking.

He glanced at the windows of his ex-wife's house again, then determinedly opened his work. The top three folders were labeled with the names of suburban Detroit hospitals—Beauregard, St. Francis, and Randolph. All three hospitals had a history of superior care until recently, when they'd had a sudden rash of lawsuits, all related to rare medical problems affecting newborns.

Traditionally even the word *newborn* invoked a panic flight response in Jake—yeah, he'd had one. He still remembered the night Danny had been born fifteen years ago—and his keeling over on his nose. So babies weren't normally his favorite subject.

But he'd accidentally come across one of these mysterious lawsuits when he'd been researching a separate story for the newspaper, and then couldn't shake his curiosity. Every question led to another dropped ash—a lit ash—and no one else seemed aware there was an incendiary pile of embers in the forest.

In itself, the increase in lawsuits didn't necessarily mean beans, because everybody sued for everything today. People especially freaked when something happened to a baby—what parent didn't suffer a rage of pain when their kid didn't come out normal? Although Jake was no longer a practicing lawyer, he knew the system. Knew how lawsuits worked.

He'd already told himself not to get so stirred up. What looked like a Teton could still end up an anthill. But it smelled wrong, this sudden burst of lawsuits—and this sudden burst of serious health problems for babies, especially when the affected hospitals had longstanding excellent reputations.

Momentarily a woman's face pounced in his mind. Kasey. Graham Crandall's wife. Crandall was one of those starched-spine controlling types—a silver-tongued snob, Jake had always thought, the kind of guy who'd give you the shirt off his back—as long as you gave him a medal for doing it. There was no trouble between them, no bad history. Jake didn't care about him one way or another, even back in the years when he'd hung with the Grosse Pointe crowd.

But it had been a shock to meet Crandall's wife. Coming out of the hospital that night, he'd only seen a woman in labor—she was crying. Who wouldn't? About to give birth to a watermelon? Yet her face kept popping in his mind. The short, rusty-blond hair. The freckled nose and sunburned cheeks.

She wasn't elegant or beautiful or anything like the women Jake associated with Crandall. Instead, there was a radiance about her, a glow from the inside, a natural joyful spirit. The wide mouth was built for laughter; her eyes were bluer than sky.

Pretty ridiculous, to remember all those details of a woman he didn't know from Adam—and a woman who was married besides. Jake figured he must have had that lightning-pull toward her for the obvious reason. It had momentarily scared him, to realize she was going into that hospital to have a baby—the same hospital where he'd been researching the lawsuits.

Now, though, he sighed impatiently and turned back to his papers. Kasey was none of his business. Hell, even these lawsuits weren't. For two years, he'd tried his best to just put one foot in front of the other, pay his bills, make it through each day, be grateful that the half-assed weekly paper had been willing to give him a job. Even the research on these hospitals he was doing on the q.t., his own time.

Jake had done an outstanding job of screwing up his life. Now he was trying to run from trouble at Olympic speed. He figured there was a limit to how many mistakes a guy could make before any hope of self-respect was obliterated for good.

The instant he heard the front door slam, he looked up, and immediately hurled his briefcase into the back seat. Quick as a blink, he forgot all about lawsuits and strangers' babies. His focus lasered on the boy hiking toward the car. Just looking at Danny made him feel a sharp ache in his gut.

At fifteen, Danny had the look of the high school stud. The thick dark hair and broody dark eyes drew the girls, always had, always would. The broad shoulders and no-butt and long muscular legs added to the kid's good looks. The cutoffs hanging so low they hinted at what he was most proud of, the cocky posture, the I-own-the-world bad-boy swagger…oh yeah, the girls went for him.

Jake should know. He'd looked just like the kid at fifteen. But there were differences.

Last week Danny's hair had been straggly and shoulder-length; this week it had colored streaks. The kid's scowl was as old as a bad habit and his eyes were angry—all the time angry, it seemed. The swagger wasn't assumed for the sake of impressing the girls, but because Danny was ready to take on anyone who looked at him sideways.

Jake understood a lot about attitude. What knifed him in the gut, though, was knowing that his son's bad attitude was his fault.

The boy yanked open the driver's door and hurled his long skinny body in the driver's seat. "You're late."

Not only was Jake ten minutes early, but he'd been waiting. Still, he didn't comment. If Danny hadn't started the conversation with a challenge, Jake would probably have had a heart attack from shock. "You brought your permit? And you told your mom that you're going out with me?"

"Like I need to be treated like a five-year-old." Danny fussed with the key, the dials, then muttered, "If I had any choice—just so we both know where we stand—I'd rather be anywhere but here."

That about said it all. Danny wanted to drive so badly that he was even willing to spend time with his dad—and then, only because no one else wanted to practice-drive with him. Even his mother valued her life too much to take the risk.

"I suppose you're in a hurry." Danny used his favorite world-weary tone as he started the car.

"Nope. I've got as much time as you want—although I assume your mom wants you back by dinner."

"Yeah. Maybe. Can I go on the expressway today?"

Maybe Churchill thought there was nothing to fear but fear itself, but the image of Danny on a Detroit expressway at rush hour was enough to make bile rise up Jake's throat in abject terror. The kid had just gotten his practice license. The last time he'd tried to do something as basic as making a right turn, he'd climbed over a curb. "I think you probably need to get a little more comfortable with the stick shift before we take on the expressway."

"That's what you said last week." Danny shoved the stick in Reverse, made the gear scream in pain, and then stalled out when he let up the clutch too fast. Red shot up his throat. "That wasn't my fault," he said furiously. "It's this old heap of a car. It's so old it doesn't respond to anything."

It was going to be one of their better times, Jake thought. Of course, as they aimed toward Lakeshore, the test questions began. *Can I play the radio. Can I drive by Julie Rossiter's house.* Can I this, can I that.

As far as Jake could tell, all the questions were designed to elicit a *no,* at which point Danny would instantly respond with a look of anger and disgust. Jake knew the game. He did his absolute best to say yes to any request that wasn't definably life-threatening. Sure, Danny could drive by the girl's house. Sure, he could play the radio— any station and at any volume he wanted. Jake encouraged him to drive exactly as he would be driving later, when he was alone, so he could see how distractions affected his concentration.

"Oh, yeah? Does that mean I can smoke while I drive?"

"No." Jake didn't elaborate, knowing how a lecture on smoking would be received. Besides, just then his right foot jammed on the imaginary brake and his pulse pumped adrenaline faster than a belching well. No, they hadn't hit that red Lincoln going through the intersection. No, scraping the tire against the curb wouldn't kill them. No, braking so fast they were both thrown forward didn't mean either of them were going to end up hospitalized.

"I'm going to be sixteen in another seven months," Danny said, as he turned onto Vernier.

"I know." Jake resisted holding his hand over his heart.

Suburban driving wasn't too bad, but Vernier eventually turned into Eight Mile. Eight Mile was a Real Road. The kind that tons of people actually used. Some of them might not realize how close they were to imminent death.

"So, any chance you might buy me a car?" Danny rushed on, "Mom'll never let me drive the Buick. It's uncool, anyway. But she's already warning me that I won't be able to use her car all the time. I really need wheels."

"I can't afford a car, Danny."

"You could. If you were still a lawyer. If we were still a family. If you weren't a drunk."

There now. Every one of the accusations stung like a bullet, just as his son intended. Sometimes Jake wanted a minute with his son—just one damn minute—when Danny wasn't trying to wound him.

But of course he'd earned those accusations. And all he could do now was hope that time—good meaningful time together—could start to heal that old, bad history. "Getting you a car isn't just about having enough money to buy one."

"The hell it isn't."

"Danny, come on, you're a new driver. You know that you need more practice before you'll be safe—or feel safe—on the road. It's nuts to start out with a new car before you have some experience under your belt."

"You care about being safe on the road? You used to drive drunk."

"Yeah, I did. And I hope you never do. I hope you're way smarter than me."

"That wouldn't take much." Danny made a left onto Mack, where approximately five thousand cars were speeding toward home. Horns blared when the Honda accidentally straddled two lanes. Jake reached for an antacid. Then Danny tried another jibe. "Mom's going out with some guys. Three of them, in fact."

"That's nice."

"I'll bet she's screwing at least one."

Jake understood that this comment was supposed to be another way to hurt him. Danny assumed that he still cared what Paula did. And even though Jake should have known better than to bite, he couldn't quite let this one go. "Don't use words like that about your mother."

"Oh, that's right. We're not supposed to tell the truth about anything. We just lie and pretend everything's okay, right? The way you lied about being an alcoholic. And about you and Mom staying together, that you were just going through a rough time but we'd all be fine."

Halfway through a yellow light, Danny gunned the engine and it stalled. The light turned red while they sat clogging the middle of the intersection. Sweat beaded on Jake's brow. He said, "Take it easy. The other drivers can see you, so there's no immediate danger. Just concentrate on getting the car started and going again."

On the inside, Jake marveled at the epiphany he kept getting from these practice driving sessions with Danny. You sure learned to value your life when it was constantly at risk.

Besides that—and in spite of Danny's sarcasm and surly scowls—Jake still felt the wonder of being with his son. It wasn't a given. Danny hadn't been willing to see him for most of the two years since the divorce—and God knew, that wouldn't have changed if Danny wasn't desperate to drive.

Jake realized he was riding a shaky fence. He fiercely wanted to make things right for his son, yet there seemed no parenting rule book for this deal. The kid was always egging him on, pushing him to lose his temper. What was the right dad-thing to do? Be tough? Or be understanding? Give him the tongue-lashing he was begging for, or keep proving to the kid that he'd never vent temper on him?

Hard questions surfaced every time they were together.

Jake didn't mind the kid beating up on him—hell, he had a lot to make up for. But just once in his life, he'd like some answers. Some *right* answers. He was already a pro at the other kind.

When Danny turned again, aiming down a side road toward Lakeshore, the boy suddenly muttered, "Julie's house is down here."

Abruptly the kid slowed to a five-mile-an-hour crawl—which was fine by Jake—until Danny made another left. Four homes down from Sacred Julie's house was the Crandall place. Jake spotted a BMW pulling into the driveway. Saw Graham Crandall climb out of the driver's seat. Saw the passenger door open.

And there was Kasey.

His pulse bucked like a stallion's in spring—just like it had the first time he'd seen her. The kick of hormones struck him as incontestable proof that a man had no brain below his waist…still, it made him want to laugh. The last time he remembered that kind of zesty hormonal kick, he'd been sixteen, driving Mary Lou Lowrey home from a movie, and 51% sure from the way she kissed him that she was going to let him take her bra off. Second base was hardly a home run, but sixteen-year-old boys were happy with crumbs. Even the promise of crumbs. At that age, the thrum of anticipation alone was more than worth living for.

Hormones were undeniably stupid, but damn. They made a guy feel busting-high alive and full of himself—a sensation Jake hadn't enjoyed in a blue moon and then some.

Temporarily his son diverted him from the view—primarily because he was doing something to torture both the gears and the brakes simultaneously. "Danny, what are you trying to do?"

Danny shot him an impatient look. "Parallel park, obviously."

"Ah." Perhaps it should have been obvious. They'd edged up the curb, down the curb, up on the stranger's grass, down on the grass, several times now. Ahead of them was a freshly washed SUV, behind them a satin-black Audi. In principle there was an ample ten feet between the cars. "Try not to go quite so close—"

"Well, this is hard," Danny groused. "How the hell are you supposed to know where the back end of another car is if you can't see it?"

But he could see her. Kasey, climbing out of the passenger seat, holding a small pink blanket. She hit him exactly the same way she had before—as if he were suffering the dizzying, stupefying effect of a stupid pill.

The darn woman wasn't any prettier than she'd been the first time. No makeup. Her rusty-blond hair was wildly tousled. She was wearing some god-awful green print that overwhelmed her delicate features. But the details just didn't matter.

The sound of her laughter pealed down the street. She didn't laugh like a lady; she laughed as if her whole heart and belly were into it, joyful laughter, the kind of hopeless giggling that it sucked in strangers passing by.

And the way she held the baby, it was damn obvious the kid was worth more than diamonds to her. As Graham crossed the car to her side, she climbed out, then surged up on tiptoe and kissed him. She looked up at him with a love so radiant and full that you'd think Graham was everything a woman ever dreamed of in a guy.

And there it was, Jake mused wryly. He got it, the reason he had such a hard time looking away from her. It was plain old jealousy.

He knew damn well no one had ever looked at him like that.

No one's fault for that but him. He'd grown up a spoiled

rich kid, raised to be selfish, to feel entitled, to take whatever he wanted whenever he wanted it. God knew his parents only meant to love him, but that upbringing had still skewed his perspective. It had taken his losing everything for Jake to figure out what mattered. He'd run out of time. Either he got around to developing some character, or he was going to end up lost for good.

An alcoholic—at least an alcoholic who was serious about recovering—discovered certain things about life. There were things you couldn't do. Other people could. You couldn't. Life was as simple and mean as that. No one else had your exact list, but Jake knew what was written on the forbidden side of his sheet. Being attracted to a married woman—a very, very married woman—was as off-limits as it got.

He understood Kasey's tug on him. Something about her reminded him of what he once thought life could be—when he still believed in dreams, when he still believed in himself, when every moment of sunshine was a treasure. He understood—but he turned off the volume and the vision, promptly.

Danny had given up trying to parallel park. He took the first left turn, aiming back toward his mother's house. He didn't speed. His driving problems had never been about carelessness, but about having no natural sense for the stick shift and the car. The more impatient he got with himself, the more he tended to make mistakes. Jake tried to shut up. Time and experience were the answers, not carping. Besides, dads couldn't die from nerves, could they?

Danny accidentally hit the gas, pulling into Paula's driveway, tried to recover by slamming on the brakes, and then, of course, stalled. For the first time in almost two hours, the kid looked him straight in the eye.

"I suppose you don't have time to do this again on Thursday," he said disgustedly.

"I suppose I do."

It probably hurt the kid like a sore, but hope surged in those broody blue eyes. "Same time? Four o'clock?"

"I may be a little late."

"Yeah, so what's new? The question is whether you'll show at all, just because you say you will."

Jake said easily, "Damn right. You think I don't know how much I need to make up for, Sport, you're mistaken. And in the meantime, if you also want to take on a drive on Saturday or Sunday—there's less traffic early in the morning, so we could go for a longer trek."

"You mean get up early?" Danny's tone suggested that particular idea was as appealing as a snake bite.

"No sweat if you don't want to. I just know you're hot to get more driving hours in, and I can't get here during the work week until after four. Weekend mornings could give us more time."

Danny heaved out of the car. "I'll think about it."

"Okay." Jake got out, too, and crossed to the other side, conscious that his son hadn't used the word *Dad,* much less said anything as pleasant as "goodbye." This lesson, though, had been significantly more peaceful than the last one. Danny hadn't sworn at him. Hadn't hit anything.

"Hey." Danny stopped at the front door, key in the lock, turning back to offer one last belligerent look.

"Yeah?" Jake assumed the "hey" was meant as some kind of question.

"Thanks for taking me," Danny said stiffly, and then promptly disappeared in the house and slammed the door.

Well, hell. Jake was stunned speechless. The kid had actually thanked him? Maybe, just maybe, father and son did have a chance to mend their fences. Of course, earning the kid's respect was still an uphill battle.

SPOTLIGHT

*"Julie Elizabeth Leto always delivers
sizzling, snappy, edge stories!"*
—New York Times *bestselling author Carly Phillips*

USA TODAY bestselling author

Julie Elizabeth Leto

Making Waves

Celebrated erotica author Tessa Dalton
has a reputation for her insatiable
appetite for men—any man. But in
truth, her erotic stories are inspired
by personal fantasies...fantasies that
are suddenly fulfilled when she meets
journalist Colt Granger.

July

HOT Bonus
Features!

Author Interview,
Bonus Read
and Romantic Beaches
off the Beaten Path

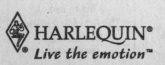

HARLEQUIN®
Live the emotion™

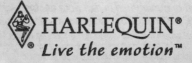